DEAD BUT STILL TICKING

(A Buckeye Barrister Mystery)

by

David M. Selcer

For information, email **Cozy Cat Press,**
cozycatpress@aol.com or visit our website at:
www.cozycatpress.com

COZY CAT
P R E S S

ISBN: 978-1-939816-05-4
Printed in the United States of America

Cover design by Nicole at Cover Shot Creations
www.covershotcreations.com

1 2 3 4 5 6 7 8 9 10

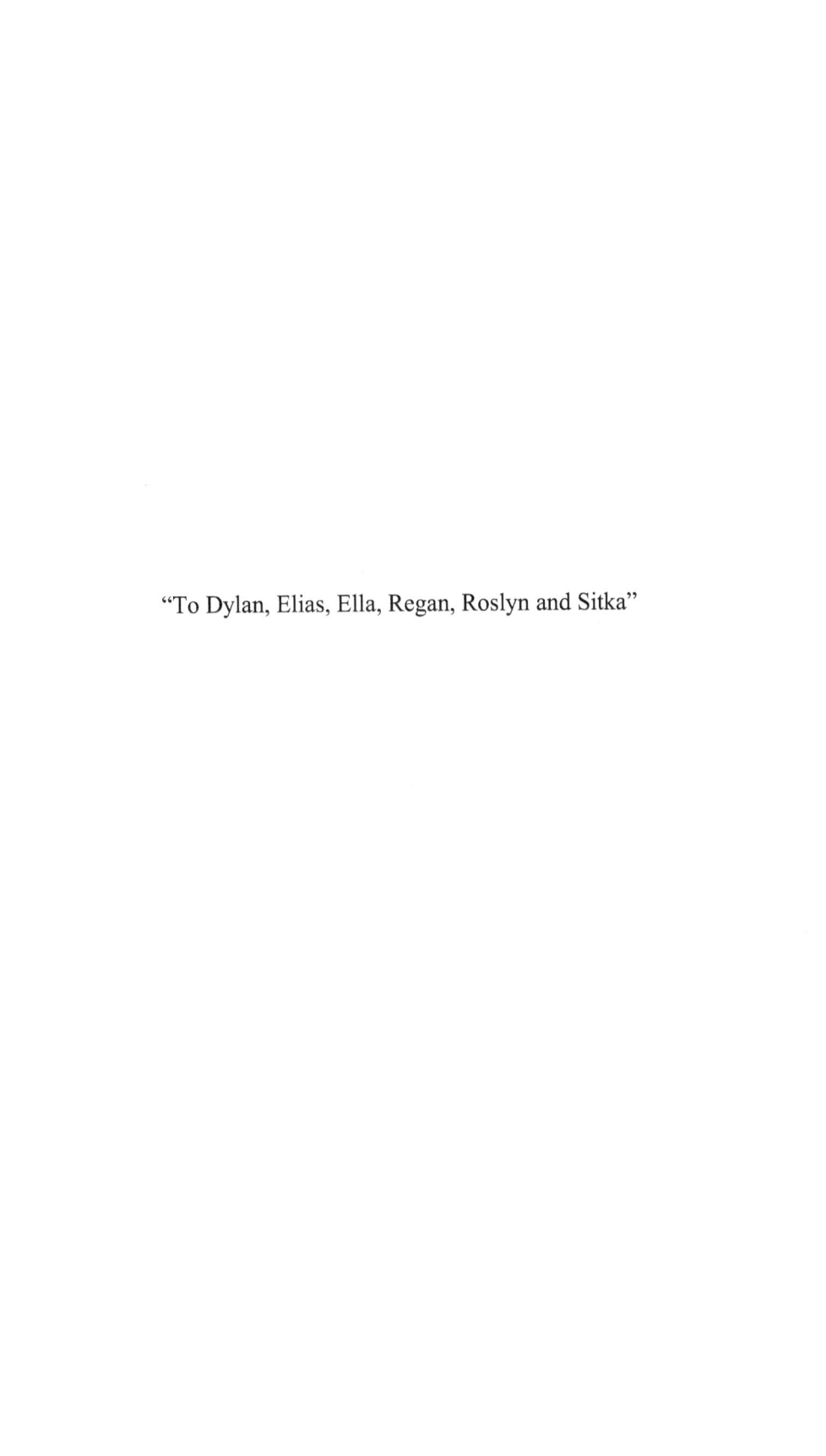

"To Dylan, Elias, Ella, Regan, Roslyn and Sitka"

Chapter One

The postman knows how un-busy my law office is by the sparseness of my mail. Here he comes now, only three pieces: another bill from the electric company, a copy of a legal periodical, and a strange envelope, return address—"The Stanley Meltzer Law Firm, Ten West Broad Street, Columbus, Ohio 43215." If I don't receive a client check for another five days, I'm shuttering the--

" Oh my god! Marinda! Look at this!"

Marinda's my legal secretary (part-time, three days a week). Before that she was a Mollie Maid who cleaned my office. Inside the Meltzer envelope was a money order, drawn on *La Banque Postale* in the amount of five million ($5,000,000) dollars, payable to Winston Barchrist III. That's me!

"What's *La Banque Postale?*" Marinda was peering over my shoulder, nonchalantly trying to ignore the amount of the check.

"I think it's the French Post office!"

"Where'd this come from?"

I detached the note clipped to the check and showed it to her. There, in the familiar handwriting of Robert Steinglass, were the words, *"Meet me at noon today for lunch and an explanation,--the Claremont, Bob S."*

"Well, heck--we're getting rich around here, Mr. B, but Rosanne isn't going to be happy if you do that."

"Do what?"

"Meet Bob Steinglass at the Claremont instead of going to Weight Watchers today."

I had a bet with Rosanne about whether I could drop 30 pounds, to be decided in a 12:00 noon weigh-in at Weight Watchers this afternoon. She had ignored the slab of flab impression I make for too long now, and I knew it bothered her. Once, taking her hand in mine I'd joked that it looked like the Santa Maria docking with the Queen Mary, but she hadn't laughed. Instead, she mentioned that there was always Weight Watchers if it bothered me. So I bet her I could lose 30 pounds.

"Which should I put first Marinda--my girl friend, or this seven figure check?"

"Oh, she's your girl friend now?"

"Well, I . . . we . . . "

"It's Ok. I don't want to hear it, boss. Did you lose the 30 pounds?

"Marinda, don't answer your own question with another question. Just call her please, and tell her something's come up."

"No, You didn't lose it, did you? In fact, you haven't lost any weight at all, right?"

I glanced down at the polar bear gut wearing my white shirt, trying to think up an explanation for failing to count up all those Weight Watchers points everyday so I would know the calorie difference between a Philly sub-sandwich and tuna salad on a bed of lettuce. Going to the Claremont instead of to Weight Watchers was going to piss Rosanne off, but I'd only dropped 6 pounds, and that would piss her off even more.

Marinda apologized for her little inquisition into my personal life, realizing it had caught me in the emotional solar-plexus.

"I'm sorry boss. It's just that you weigh over 300 pounds, and if you keel over from a heart attack or something, I'm out of a job. It's not because I like you or anything. You know that. No problem, right?"

"No problem, Marinda. I just feel an allegiance to Robert Steinglass."

Robert Steinglass is my only true lawyer buddy in Columbus. I met him on my first day back in the city, after what I call "The Great Catastrophe." I won't bore you with details of "The Great Catastrophe." Suffice it to say, it happened in Chicago while I was practicing law there, and it almost led to my disbarment. I was a young associate at one of the premier securities law firms in the "Second City," --now, the third city, after Los Angeles—and I made a non-disclosure mistake, which is a big no-no in securities law. Ultimately, I didn't lose my license, because the mistake was my supervising partner's fault, but the disruption caused me to lose everything else—my wife, my new baby, my job, my self-confidence . . . just about everything of any value to me. I needed to escape Chicago and forget it all.

So I interviewed for positions in a tertiary city, Columbus, Ohio. You know it's a tertiary city when you have to say the state it's in after you say the name of the city. For instance, you don't just say Selma. You say Selma, Alabama.

Anyways, when I met Robert he was a new partner working for Stanley Meltzer, probably the best securities lawyer in Columbus-- at least that's how Stanley liked to think of himself. Other law firms bore the names of all their partners, or at least their lead partners, but not Stanley's. He preferred simply to call his shop The Stanley Meltzer Law Firm. Everybody encouraged me to try out for his team, the "foremost securities boutique in the Midwest," they all called his office.

So I sent him my resume. Why Columbus? I went to law school here. I was married here. So I was sort of like the prodigal son returning home with his tail between his legs.

Stanley invited me to Columbus for a visit, without mentioning who was going to pay my travel expenses. That should have been a tip off. When he walked in and saw all 300 pounds of me sitting there waiting to be interviewed, he took one look and he said, "You'll have to excuse me today, Mr. Barker, but something positively important is claiming my attention."

"Barchrist, not Barker," I replied to his departing back. He didn't bother to tell me what would be happening next, or whether I should just show myself out. A minute later Robert Steinglass entered the room and sat down. Bob didn't have my resume with him, but he also didn't act disinterested. He spent almost an hour with me. Throughout our meeting, he never stopped smiling, keeping his eyes on mine all the time, carefully answering all of my questions, but never asking me any. There was something about him I liked, and I still like it to this day. I finally asked him if there was anything he wanted to know about me. That's when we got down to some real talking.

"So what brings you to Columbus looking for a job?" he asked.

"Well, I went to Ohio State Law School, and things in Chicago, well . . . they . . ." I began stammering.

"I know all about the Barchrist case," he interrupted. "Tough break! Life just has a way of throwing its curve balls at us, doesn't it?"

What was the Barchrist case? Well, in short, after fouling up that securities prospectus I was drafting for my Chicago firm's biggest client, I got sued. Actually, I didn't miss anything. I was told, by the partner overseeing my work, that a 10 million dollar charge against a multibillion dollar corporation's earnings for a recently discovered fraud in the sale of insurance policies was immaterial because the amount was mere "chump" change to a company that size, and it wouldn't effect shareholder value.

"We don't want to tic them off at us, do we—not a client this big?" He explained. So I became the "chump," by not disclosing it.

Instead, we ticked off the stockholders and the Supreme Court, which saw the issue a little differently than my boss, in a class action law suit captioned *SEC v. Winston Barchrist III, et al,* The *et al.* included my law firm, the CPAs, and the underwriters, but the world never knew that, because the case is always just cited as *SEC vs. Barchrist, et al.* I was included on principle only, to show that the SEC's disclosure rules apply to everyone, "even the lowliest associate of a large law firm," to quote the Court's opinion. That little nod to propriety ruined my career as a securities lawyer.

"So I guess the lawsuit's the real reason Mr. Meltzer didn't want to bother with me," I said to Robert.

"Doubtful," he replied. "It's more likely he was put off by your girth. You're quite heavy, you know. Stanley Meltzer is meticulous in every respect. I'm sure he knew all about the Barchrist case before he invited you to interview here, and that he was nonetheless very impressed with your credentials, and felt you would be a good addition to his securities law business. That's what he thinks of it as, you know—not a law practice, but a business. But a man like Stanley's not willing to take the risk that the looks of one of his lawyers might offend a client, even a lawyer he plans on keeping in the back room."

I took a look at Robert as he was talking. He was a beautiful man, indeed, in every respect, and dressed to the hilt. "So, I guess that's it for me and the Stanley Meltzer firm, huh?"

"Don't let it bother you," he replied. "Set up your own shop. Go into practice for yourself. Take any case that comes through the door for a while. I'll help you, and so will my friends. You'll see."

"But there are um-teen other business law firms in town, and I've got interviews set up with a lot of them."

"Take it from me," Robert said. "Go into practice for yourself. Don't waste your time. You're in the hinterlands now, where people are evaluated more on how they look, than how they are. It's not what you know, but what you show. It's not how smart you are, but whether you can shoot par. If you wait to have interviews with all those firms, someday maybe you'll get a job with one of them, not because of your credentials, but because you'll have lost so much weight from starving while you wait, that you'll look better." He smiled tentatively.

He was right. I was a brontosaurus trying to look like an Ivy Leaguer. I had 15 more interviews without one bite. So I settled for practicing as a single practitioner, chasing ambulances and divorces. Bob's a friend, because he's a straight shooter, and he told me the truth. He's also as good as his word. He sent me many clients when I opened my general law practice, because he had many friends. I mean lots.

Robert's gay. He deals daily in the higher echelons of finance, where most of the people are either straight, or too absorbed to figure out what they are. But, he lives privately in the world of the Doo-Dah parade, an annual Fourth of July event in Columbus for gays.

So what! His gay friends have just as many car wrecks, collections, domestic violence cases, real estate matters, DUI's, and, yes, divorces, separations and annulments, as anybody else. The only difference is, if you're a friend of Robert's, they trust you to be their lawyer.

The Claremont is Robert's favorite place. Going there used to be real torture for me. In the past, I'd always felt out of place in this atmosphere, like a carp in an aquarium filled with tropical pin fish, or a bowling ball trying to fit into a pool table pocket. It was always filled with lawyers politicians and business people in pin striped suits who knew each other well, sitting and *kibitzing,* while I sat alone in my plaid sport jacket, not knowing anybody. They say if you want to find anything out, just go to the Claremont Restaurant and listen to the rumors flying around, but I never heard anything while I was there, because nobody ever talked to me. So I rarely ate there—really, only when I needed to pump a bailiff or some other court official about how a judge was going to manage one of my cases on his docket.

But things were a little different for me now at the Claremont. I walked in early, feeling pretty good about myself this time. Wearing the new suit Rosanne made me buy, navy, without pin stripes, to thin me out as much as possible, I looked as good as I could look. And, instead of using my old mode of transportation— the moped—I'd driven over in the new Toyota Avalon, with leather, I'd bought with the money I'd recently earned on my first big case—the Ledraque Trust matter. As a result of that engagement, many of the lawyers in town who eat lunch at the Claremont, actually now know who I am. The case had been all over the pages of the Columbus Dispatch. The trust was being misused to pay off an Ohio State football player for throwing games, and I had discovered it.

"What'll it be this afternoon Mr. Barchrist?" the waitress said. She actually knew my name!

"Oh, just a *Sauvignon Blanc,*" I replied, fighting the urge to say "nothing thanks," and save money. Humph—I had a $5,000,000 check back at the office, and here I was, thinking of saving money. But I knew one had to have a drink in front of himself while waiting for a meet-up at the Claremont. *It's not what you know, but what you show*, Robert always said. He was late—very unusual for him. Anyway, there weren't that many calories in one *Sauvignon Blanc*.

I watched the entrance to the restaurant filling up, as people crowded in looking for their luncheon partners. I couldn't help thinking that there must have been a mistake. Robert would probably show up and tell me he put the wrong check in the envelope or something. A banker, came in and nodded to me—probably thought that I now represented the Ledraque Trust and would have some sway over where it took its business. Maybe that was it! The $5,000,000 was actually an amount to be held in trust for somebody but the word "trustee" had been omitted after my name. Two lawyers, who also came in, acknowledged me, willing, finally, to greet me as a fellow member of the Columbus Bar, now that my picture had appeared all over the paper in connection with unraveling the biggest trust scam in the State. I didn't know their names, but they knew mine. So they winked and nodded their heads to me as they passed.

Jerry Shapiro walked in, followed by Detective Anthony Picard. Jerry's actually the beat cop for the area, and he's also a friend, which is not an easy relationship, because he can be very obnoxious. His usual *modus operandi*, is to pull his cruiser up as close as he can to the front door of whatever establishment he's entering, and just park it there, sometimes leaving his pursuit lights running. It tends to pretty much ruin the solemnity of any place.

He was wearing his uniform and gun, but not particularly trying to exude any sort of police presence today, which is unusual for him. Antoine Picard works downtown, and he's low key, but a decent detective. They both helped me crack the Ledraque case.

The two of them clearly had only come in for lunch, but almost immediately they were mobbed by lawyers waiting to be seated—very strange. I wondered what it was all about, because usually Picard was quiet and retiring, unlike his lunch mate. Now, however, he was holding up his hands, palms out above his head, as if trying to say that he didn't know anything. Shapiro kept trying to move everyone back from the detective, practicing his crowd control techniques. But the questions kept coming and Picard kept refusing to answer. Suddenly, Officer Shapiro spotted me, left his brother cop stuck at the door with the petite mob, and, came over to my table.

"Hey counselor," he blurted, smiling. Effusiveness wasn't really Jerry's style, so his greeting seemed out of place. "What brings you into the Forum today? Looking for something in particular, or just basking in the light of your former headlines?"

Every other sentence out of Jerry's mouth bordered on putting down whomever he was talking to. He didn't even know he was doing it.

"The Forum?" I asked quizzically.

"You know, I mean like 'the Roman Forum,'" he responded, as if I needed to get with it. "When you come to the Claremont, you're going out in public, man. It's like going out into the old Roman Forum. You're among the people here. Just look at you there, wearing your new navy toga."

"Oh, Oh, Oh," I answered, as if I knew what he was talking about. "Rosanne picked this suit out for me."

"Yah, but you chose to wear it here. How's come? Usually you're in that motley plaid jacket of yours. Makes you look like a huge glom of tic tac toe games."

He laughed and bumped my upper arm with his fist. "Just kidding! Hah, hah."

"I'm meeting Bob Steinglass for lunch," I replied, wondering what business that was of my nosey obnoxious cop friend.

"Oh, my God," he replied. "Haven't you heard?"

"What?" I asked indignantly.

"Robert Steinglass is dead—cause unknown! His cleaning lady found him in his apartment this morning. The place was a real mess! Furniture toppled and papers strewn everywhere, but not a mark on him. Murder's suspected, of course, but his family won't even allow an autopsy. They want him buried fast, for religious reasons or something"

I downed the rest of my *Sauvignon Blanc* with one gulp.

"Still always a half step behind the times, aren't you counselor?" Shapiro quipped.

Chapter Two: A Rightful Heir

"There's a Mr. Anthony Basheer out there to see you," Marinda announced, entering my office. She didn't use the telephone intercom. That would never occur to her unless I'd told her to use it, at least as often as every morning. But I was glad. It was always a pleasure to watch Marinda exit a room.

I was still getting over the shock of yesterday's news. The horror of Bob's questionable death was like a blanket covering me, and a lot of others in the Columbus legal community. The only difference was, none of them had just received an inexplicable check for $5,000,000 from him, with a promise to explain, which he could now never fulfill.

Anthony Basheer didn't have an appointment, but I knew who he was. He wasn't a client. In fact, it was rare that anyone actually showed up at the dilapidated office I maintained above a Dairy Mart on Whittier Avenue in South German Village. Over and over, I'd requested Marinda to ask all telephone callers, "May I tell Mr. Barchrist what this is in reference to?" I even had it written down on the permanent to-do list she kept at her desk. So you'd think that when somebody unexpected like Basheer actually showed up, she'd ask...but nooo—oh, noo! If it was a new situation, in any tiny way, Marinda didn't know what to do.

Tony Basheer was the last person I wanted to see, especially without knowing why he'd come in. He was a dancer in Columbus's nascent Ballet Met Company, and he'd been a fraternity brother of Robert Steinglass's at the University of Michigan, in Tau Delta Phi. He was also a Lebanese Christian, born in the town of Jbail, just north of Beirut, and the only Arab in a Jewish fraternity. He was extremely artsy, performing in all the big campus productions during his college days, and he compelled reactions from almost everyone he encountered, because of his quick humor and relentless engagement. He had dark hair, dark eyes and was always intense. He was also Robert Steinglass's lover— ex-lover now. He walked into my office bereft, almost faint, as he dramatically collected himself, fighting to hold back tears.

"Robert meant a lot to me," he blithered, taking my outstretched hand and placing it on his breast. The move was dramatic, and I didn't know what to do. Rosanne would have known, but there was no way to get a hold of her at the moment.

I put my arm around his shoulder trying to comfort him, thinking I must have looked like a behemoth comforting a nymph. He was small, like a woman, in my arms.

"I know, I know. I'm so sorry Tony," I said. "Please accept my condolences. What can I do for you?"

"You can get me my fair share," he whined, looking up into my eyes. "That bastard he called his partner is already trying to act like I don't exist."

"What bastard?"

"Stanley Meltzer!"

"What do you mean?"

"What do I mean? I mean Robert had a partnership interest in a very lucrative law firm. Robert left no heirs other than me. But Stanley Meltzer is already acting as if the partnership never was. When I called on him at his office to talk about it, he wouldn't even see me."

Tony began crying again. "He's obliterated all evidence that the partnership ever existed—literally obliterated it! Robert's name is gone from his door, and it's only been two days. His office has been completely emptied, and somebody new is already in there. The firm stationery has already been changed. Robert's phone is disconnected and all his clients have been reassigned. The name on his parking space has been painted over. There's not a trace of Robert left! Why? Stanley's even had his name dropped from the Columbus Bar Association's rolls."

"Why would Stanley Meltzer do something like that?" I asked.

"Well—because he doesn't want to have to settle up with the likes of me, silly!"

This was not a spat I particularly wanted to get into. Robert was my friend and Tony was his lover, but Tony was not necessarily my friend, and I didn't relish representing him in this kind of case. "Did Robert have a will?" I inquired.

"Yes."

"Did he leave you his partnership interest?"

"The will says he leaves me all his property. He made me the executor of his estate. I haven't seen it, but he told me that's what it says."

Perfect, I thought to myself—*just perfect! After finally starting to get some traction as a member of the Columbus legal community, now I was going to have to represent a male ballet dancer in a fight with one of the city's most celebrated members of the bar over his business relationship with Robert and the terms of a will...*

"Well, then, bring the will in. We should file it with the Probate Court." I said tentatively.

"I don't have the will. It's locked up in the safe at the Stanley Meltzer law firm."

"What about a copy?"

"I don't have a copy! Oh, Winston. I'm such a fool! When Robert told me about the will, he tried to give me a copy. But I couldn't bear the thought of him dying, so I wouldn't take it. Why am I always so unrealistic? That shouldn't make any difference though, should it? Robert and I were married in San Francisco last year during that brief period when gay marriages were legalized in California. Did you know we got married? So, don't I inherit automatically under something called the Statute of Decent and Distribution?"

Well, nobody's being unrealistic here, I thought to myself! *That should just make his inheritance a lead pipe lock. After all, the law's the law isn't it? The spouse takes half under the Statute of Descent and Distribution, and a spouse is a spouse, even if the same sex as the deceased? Right? What a perfect opportunity this was going to be to discredit myself with the Columbus Bar and the courts, now that I'd finally gained a little respect with them.*

"Tony, let me ask, who do you think could have done this thing to Robert? Did he have enemies? Was he depressed? Could he have done himself in? Where were you when it happened?"

Right away, I realized the last question was the wrong thing to ask. It was a question I knew the police would be asking, and that's where the investigation of Robert's death belonged—in the police station.

"Where was I? WHERE WAS I? I was in Detroit over the weekend, specifically in Dearborn. That's where!"

I knew the Detroit area had the largest Arab community in the United States. It was practically an Arab city, full of Arab bookstores, grocery outlets, restaurants and sweetshops. It even had its own Arab radio and television programs, political parties, nightclubs, and Arabic language schools. About 300,000 Arabs populated the city from all over the Middle East—Lebanese, Syrians, Chaldeans from Iraq, Palestinians, Jordanians and Yemenis. With the exception of Sao Paulo, in Brazil, Detroit is considered the largest Arab city outside of the Arab World. Tony Basheer would have felt very welcome there.

"On the day of Robert's death," I continued, "I received a mysterious money order in the amount of $5,000,000 with a note from him to meet him at the Claremont for an explanation. Do you know anything about that?"

"Not really." Tony pulled a scrap of paper from his pocket with a telephone number on it. "Call this number. Maybe you'll find out something."

"Why?"

"I don't know why. DON'T ASK ME WHY! Why ask me something like that? The number was just on the dresser, and I know he called it many times talking about money, and it may have some connection with the money order you received. Once, I heard him say over the phone that he'd deliver some money to you, as soon as he received it, but I don't know who he was talking to at the time. The money must have come in the mail to the apartment the weekend I was in Detroit. Just call the number. You want the five million, don't you?"

It sounded like Tony knew more than he was telling me, but I didn't want to press him. The number was an international phone number, with a country code and city code on it. I picked up the phone to check it out with AT&T and they told me the country code was for France, and the city code was one of the many Paris city codes. It was two o'clock in the morning in Paris. The call would have to wait.

"They say it looked almost like a mob killing," I said returning my attention to Robert's possible murder. Tony began sobbing again, but made no comment.

"Ok," I told him. "Obviously, you've got enough on your mind, and you don't need any more prying from me. You came here about Robert's will, and I'll agree to visit Stanley Meltzer's office for you, and ask him to see if the will's in his safe and whether you're the executor. If he won't cooperate, we'll file a probate action and get a subpoena."

"Maybe this will help," Tony said, pulling an envelope from his pocket. The envelope contained a letter from Robert to Tony, dated a week prior. It chastised Tony for being foolish about refusing to accept a copy of the will, and stated that the original was in the safe at the Stanley Meltzer Law Firm. It went on to state that if anything ever happened to him, Tony should go there to get it, and then come to see me because I'd know what to do.

"This letter was written very recently," I said, astonished. "It's almost as if Robert was expecting something to happen to him. If you know more than you're telling me, Tony, now would be the best time to let it out. What was Robert doing that would cause him to write a letter like this at this time? Who had he been in contact with recently? What were his dealings? Come on. You were his lover, and I know you know more than you're telling me. Lovers always do."

Tony's wet face reddened, almost as if something was trying to come out of his mouth that he didn't want to let out. He began pacing my office like a metronome—precise steps, back and forth. He took out a handkerchief and blew his nose. He was sweating now.

"All I know is that he had some sort of business with the Waqf. It might be about that."

"The Waqf? What's the Waqf?"

"You Westerners really don't know a thing about the Arab World do you? All you know is your Vatican, your Jewish Federations, and your United Ways"

"Well, what is it?"

A Waqf is a charity but more. It's a permanent dedication of something for any purpose recognized by Sharia law as religious, pious or charitable."

"Oh, like a foundation. I understand."

"But more than that—it's like a foundation in perpetuity. There are many Waqfs. They're like trusts."

"Well, which one was Robert dealing with?" I asked.

"I don't know," Toni said. "Call the telephone number I gave you. Maybe you'll find out."

"Ok, I will. In the meantime, when and where is the funeral?"

"Oh that's a big secret too. Nobody will tell me. What family he has, certainly won't. Homophobic prigs! They're just planning a small private burial, 'family only.' You know how that goes—attendance by invitation." He broke down in tears again.

Chapter Three: Where Do I Pay My Respects?

I called Billy Goldman from my car. Billy's my rabbi, even though I'm not Jewish, and Billy's also a former client who introduced me to Rosanne. Robert was Jewish, and I thought maybe Billy could help me find out where he was going to be buried and when.

"Maybe I can. Maybe I can't," Rabbi Goldman said, carefully weighing my question as if committing to answer it would be painful for him. You see," he said, "the Jewish funeral director in Columbus and I haven't been on the best of terms, ever since I secretly buried a convert in the Orthodox Jewish Cemetery next to her husband. The funeral director thought she was a *shiksa* because she hadn't undergone her conversion with an Orthodox Rabbi. I told him not to be such a stickler, that Ruth in the Bible, was a *shiksa* too, and she turned out almost to be a matriarch, but he wanted to be a *schmuck* about it. So he doesn't talk to me. Frankly, I don't get it. You know they're all dead anyway."

Ruth who?"

"You know—Ruth, the Moabite who married Boaz, a relative of Naomi's—in the Bible? She was a *shiksa* who married a Jew, but after Boaz died, she told Naomi, 'Wherever you go, I will go...where you die, I will die. There I will be buried,' etc., etc. Supposedly, she was King David's great grandmother."

Billy never hesitated to punctuate a conversation with references to the Old Testament, probably because he'd only learned it seven years ago, when he'd run away to a yeshiva in Israel after doing six months on a charge of fencing criminal goods. Before that, he was operating a pawn shop, but when he got out of jail, he decided to become a rabbi, and he enticed me into joining his Sunday study group by introducing me to Rosanne. "Rosanne's not a *shiksa*, but she's got fabulous legs," he told me.

"Will you get back to me on this, Billy?" I asked. "I want to go to Bob's funeral."

"Winston, is the Pope Catholic? Shaa-lom," Billy always emphasized the first syllable of the word shalom for some reason when he said it to me.

Within five minutes he called back. "Funeral's in Fremont, Ohio, where Robert Steinglass was born," he reported. "It's going to be today at 4:00 p.m. The Steinglass's are the only Jewish family up there. They're bringing in a rabbi from the Elyria/Loraine area to do the service. It's going to be very small, and hush-hush, I get the impression."

"Thanks, Rabbi. I've heard it's supposed to be family only, but I'm going anyways. If I leave now, I've just about got enough time to make it up to Fremont. I owe it to Robert. How'd you find this information?"

"The Chevra Kaddisha."

"The heavy what?"

"Not heavy—*Chevra Kaddisha*, Winston—otherwise known as the *Committee of the Dead.* It's an organization of Jewish men and women who watch over the body of a deceased person, seeing to it that it's prepared for burial correctly and that it's not desecrated. One of the men in the group is a friend of mine."

"Man, you Jews have a committee for everything."

"Have a little respect for another religion, Winston, please."

"Rabbi," I said, trying to show more respect, "while I've got you on the phone, maybe there's something else you could do for me."

"Certainly, Winston—anything, you know that. What can I do? Do you need some counseling?"

Billy was always trying to give me solace, because he thought I still suffered from the loss of my former wife and child, in other words that I was depressed— and he was right.

"Sorry to disappoint you on that score, Billy, but I want to talk to you because you were born in Columbus, and you know the Jewish community here like the back of your hand. I need the skivvies on Stanley Meltzer. I have a meeting coming up with him—I think. What can you tell me about him?"

"His father wasn't like he is," Billy said. "Stanley Meltzer, Sr. was a real *mensch,* not that Stanley, Jr. isn't of course. Please, don't get me wrong. But the father was a *Tzedick,* a righteous man, who labored to uphold the rights of the down-trodden. He got workers paid when employers were holding out. He got pensions for the elderly. He defended my own father when the landlord tried to throw our pawn shop out of his building. He was a respected lawyer in the community.

Stanley Jr. is more, shall we say, selective in the clients he represents—only big corporations, and the wealthiest individuals. If he talks to you, it's because you've got legal business he wants. I'm not saying this is wrong, you understand. Please, don't misunderstand me. Stanley Jr. has done very well for himself, which seems to be one of the main requirements for prestige in the Jewish community these days in Columbus—well, in any community for that matter. Both he and that Ukrainian wife of his have a very high social standing.

She's going to be a very rich lady when he dies, even though I think she's a real *dybbuk*."

"And what might a *dybbuk* be?"

"It's Yiddish for a devil, an evil spirit."

"Where do you think all this leaves me, Billy?" I continued. "I'm going to be asking Stanley Meltzer, Jr. to do what's right for a gay person."

"I wish you luck, my friend. Frankly, it reminds me of the story of Ishmael and Hagar in the Bible. Abraham's only son was Ishmael, whom he had with an Egyptian slave named Hagar, until something better came along—Isaac, a son from his formerly barren wife, Sarah. At Sarah's insistence, he threw Ishmael and Hagar out. Ishmael's descendants, the Arabs, have plagued Isaac's descendants, the Jews, even down to today. Maybe you ought to tell Stanley the story when you see him. You can tell him to do the right thing to avoid future plagues, but I doubt it'll get you far."

As always, Rabbi Billy had an answer from the Old Testament, even if it didn't make complete sense at the time. I put in a call to my office, intending to leave a message on the answering machine Marinda had shamed me into buying, reminding her to make an appointment for me with Stanley Meltzer for some time next week.

Surprisingly, Marinda was there—on a Friday, no less—even though it wasn't one of her work days. She was fiercely re-typing a brief she'd completely blown on Thursday. It was due by 9:00 a.m. Monday morning. I could hear her pecking along as she tried to talk to me over the phone while she was typing, anxiously swearing a blue streak every time she hit the "r" instead of the "e," which was her biggest typing nemesis. The rheumatoid arthritis she'd been stricken with shortly after graduating from her typing class in secretarial school was acting up again. It had abbreviated her tenure with every temp service she'd tried out for, and temping was the major route to success as a legal secretary, but she just couldn't make it with any of the agencies because her arthritis ruined her typing speed.

"Marinda! I'm glad you're there. I didn't expect you'd be in. Could you please get me an appointment with Stanley Meltzer for some time next week? No, not at the Claremont—at his office."

When I'd first met Marinda, she was, leaning over the front side of my desk, in her grey cleaning service utility shorts, straining to reach my phone so she could answer it. Her well groomed brunette head, was almost obfuscated by her beautiful derrière. Her hamstrings were the prettiest I'd seen in a week.

"Hello. You've reached the office of William Barchrist, III," she'd purred into the receiver, as if I didn't exist. "No he's not. This is the cleaning service."

"If you're from the cleaning service," I asked, "why are you answering my phone?"

"Nice Bermudas," she'd replied, looking back over her perfect rump. "You must have forgotten to turn on your answering service."

I was wearing my madras Bermudas that day, because I hadn't planned to go out anywhere.

"I don't have an answering service, but if you're going to answer, for God sakes, don't tell them you're the cleaning service. How did you get in here anyways?"

"I never heard of an attorney without an answering service," she chirped from behind her ass.

"I can't afford one," I replied.

She sat up on my desk, swinging around with her arms framing her knees and resting her chin between her kneecaps in a call-girl pose. "I don't suppose you need a secretary then, do ya?" Her dark eyes flashed for a minute under her brunette curls. "Or, maybe, just a typist?"

And that was it! I'd hired her, probably because I was lonely at the time. She turned out to be the least competent, most loyal, secretary a lawyer could have.

Chapter Four: The Funeral of Robert Steinglass

Fremont, Ohio is the Walleye Capital of the World. Every spring, hundreds of fisherman crowd the banks of its Sandusky River, shoulder to shoulder, casting Erie-Dearies (multi-colored lead-weighted lures) at the steady rampage of obsessed females thrashing their way upstream to spawn. A week later, the males come. In case you don't know, a walleye's a fish. It's nothing like a buckeye, which is either a nut, or an Ohio State football fan, or maybe both.

Not exactly requiring the genteel skill of a fly fishermen, the annual Walleye-O-Rama features camper-driving sportsmen in fatigue-wear, shouting "beer me," and falling into the river at the rate of at least one per hour. These guys can't afford to hire charters to take them out on Lake Erie during its coveted Walleye Season. Instead, they leave a swath of crushed beer cans, cigarette butts, Frito bags, rubbers, broken branches and plastic mud worm containers in their wake on the lawns fronting the inlet river to Lake Erie in Sandusky County. Occasionally, turf fights even break out, because of the over-crowded fishing conditions, and the game warden has to stop checking fishing licenses long enough to call in the Sandusky County Sheriff with his paddy wagon.

Because of one of these fish riots, when I reached Fremont, it took me over an hour to get to the cemetery, which was just next to the grounds of the Rutherford B. Hayes Presidential Homestead, the only park in the city. I missed the funeral, so I wandered the grounds of the

Hayes estate. Rutherford B. Hayes was one of seven presidents born in Ohio. The other six: Ulysses S. Grant, William Howard Taft, William McKinley, Warren G. Harding, James A. Garfield and Benjamin Harrison, were all Republicans, and, except for Grant, not one of them was worth a damn. If they'd had presidential libraries, there wouldn't have been any books there about them because none were ever written.

When I reached the park, it took some time to find the cemetery. A little corner of it had an iron fence with a Jewish Star on the gate and eleven tombstones inside, inscribed in Hebrew. It was the Jewish section of the Fremont cemetery. I got out of my car, careful to keep my distance from the small group still gathered inside the fence. Not more than ten people were there, and the rabbi had already left. Suddenly, a voice startled me from behind.

"Hello, Winston. Funny, I was just thinking of calling you, and now, here you are, all the way from C-bus, as they call it. It's a sure sign that I should be contacting you again."

It was Lloyd Bruce ("Just call me Brucie"), a former client Robert had sent me a couple of years ago. I should have known then to beware of anyone with two first names, but I needed the business.

"Brucie, what are you doing here?" I inquired.

"I came to pay my respects, same as you, I suppose. Why would you ask a thing like that? You knew Robert and I were in business together. He was a partner in my new venture."

"No, no, actually I didn't know that. You mean he was in the gefilte fish business with you? I heard that business turned out to be the coup of the century, but I didn't know Bob had an interest in it."

I'd met Brucie when he wanted to buy a pig farm just outside a little southern Ohio town called Gallipolis in Gallia County, where he planned to live, build a rendering plant, make sausage, and begin producing *lerpostej*, a Scandinavian paté, made from lard and pork liver, that had a taste like the French *paté en terrine*. Brucie and I travelled down to Gallipolis, Ohio, to meet the selling pig farmer, a huge tobacco-spitting giant in his early 50s wearing jean overalls with mutton chops hanging down his cheeks from under a straw hat.

Outside of New Orleans and St. Louis, Gallipolis, Ohio, is one of the few remaining frontier settlements of French origin along the Mississippi-Ohio River Valley. The French flavor of the place persists there even today. As a nod to the past, its residents have tried to preserve its ambience by naming their offspring with French names, though long ago the area was retrofitted with West Virginian holler dwellers migrating north in search of work and welfare. Hence, people in Gallipolis have first names like Jean-Pierre (pronounced *Pee'air*) and Paul-Henri (pronounced *Awnry*), with surnames like Butts and Hairston.

We got off on the wrong foot with the Gallia County farmer immediately when Brucie stepped in a pig paddy on the farmer's front lawn, and then flounced onto his front porch, tracking it up with pig crap. As soon as Brucie opened his mouth, the farmer knew he wasn't the type who'd fit in with the other 4-H'ers in the Gallia County area—all tobacco farmers, dairy cow herders, ex-coal miners, junk yard operators, river rats and such.

"Well, what would a young good lookin' feller like you be wantin' with a pig farm down here in these parts?" he asked, punctuating the question by gnashing a chaw between his rotting brown teeth and expectorating it over his porch railing.

A beautiful suntanned, healthy looking girl, about 18, with long blond hair wildly cascading over her shoulders suddenly appeared in the doorway to join us. Barefoot and wearing cut-off jeans tight enough to make any man woozy, and a plaid cotton blouse straining over her ample bosom, she was the paradigm of the farmer's daughter.

"I want to make *paté*," my client answered the farmer excitedly.

"Wha? Pate here's my wife! Did you say what Ah think you just said? You wanna make Pate—ma wife here? Well, she ain't fer sale!" And with that, he picked up the shotgun leaning against the wall of the house, loaded it with two cartridges, and put one of them into my client's groin, straight away. "There's what you git if you want Pate," he hissed.

So, Brucie began looking elsewhere to salve his entrepreneurial itch. If the gods weren't going to favor his *paté* enterprise, he'd try something else, and he did,—gefilte fish. He also got mean, probably because the shotgun blast had pureed his groin pretty badly. Eventually, I stopped representing him, even though he was my first true business client in Ohio.

"Winston, it's good to see you again," Brucie, said, avoiding my question about Robert being in his gefilte fish business. "I'd like to have you over today, since you're here, but there's a party going on at my house that's been in progress for three days, and I don't think you'd be comfortable there. Instead, let me put you up at our local hotel and take you up to the lake tomorrow to see my newest acquisition. Can you stay? I've been thinking of using you again as my lawyer in connection with it."

"Newest acquisition? I thought you were getting rich selling product to the Chicago Kosher Kedem Company to make gefilte fish?"

Lake Erie is clogged with "Sheep Head," also known, scornfully, by charter captains as silver bass,

Catawba dolphin, groaners, and grunters, and by the only people who eat them, Louisiana Creoles, as "Gaspargou." They're a bottom feeding nuisance fish, with ugly lippy mouths, that like to catch a sports fisherman's bait before bass or walleye can get to it, and they're very fast, with ugly big fins and huge scales, but considered inedible by frustrated walleye hungry charter captains who see too many of them come over the side.

Brucie, however, knew Sheep Head were like carp, the main ingredient in gefilte fish, and that's what gave him his big idea about cornering the gefilte fish market in the United States. He ruthlessly forced Chicago Kosher Kedem into an exclusive requirements contract by threatening to disclose that some of their meats came from overruns at Muslim Halal food shop producers. Then he began paying Lake Erie Charter captains a quarter a head to bring in their Sheep Head, instead of crushing their brains out and throwing them back. It led to a huge business for him.

"I'm still in the fish business, but I've come across something much bigger," he bragged.

"So what's your newest acquisition?"

"I bought North Bass Island. C'mon, let's go see it together tomorrow. You'll enjoy."

Brucie was wearing a sport jacket over a black t-shirt with tight jeans and sandals, that made him look more like a bar bouncer than a funeral attendee. Apparently, now he was diversifying from gefilte fish into real estate. The guy was positively manic when it came to pursuing new business ventures.

"Sure," I said, thinking I had nothing to lose. I was already up near the lake anyway. "I'll go."

Chapter Five: A Day on Lake Erie

Brucie showed up at my hotel in the morning wearing a black Lido tank suit. "Here, put these on," he said, handing me an oversized pair of hunting pants and a double extra large sweat shirt with a message on the front that said "I love your lips—Blow me."

"Why would you buy North Bass Island?" I asked.

There are a number of islands in the western basin of Lake Erie, the five most well known of which are Put-In-Bay (also known as South Bass Island), Middle Bass Island (home of the Alonze Winery), North Bass Island (sometimes called Isle of St. George), and Kelly's Island, all of which are below the United States border with Canada, and Pelee Island, which is in Canada. North Bass, the smallest of these islands, is little more than a huge grape vineyard with a few houses on it.

"You'll see the attraction when we get there."

Catawba Island, which isn't really an island, is one of the main jump-off points to the Western Basin of Lake Erie. Surrounded by a plethora of bait shops, trailer parks, fish cleaning establishments, diners, gas stations and lap dancing joints, it's actually a peninsula, where the Lake Erie Ferry makes its first stop. From there, the boat traverses the roiling lake to Put-In-Bay, an historic War of 1812 site, which today doubles as a vacation spot soaked in alcohol, with beautiful bikinied bodies roasting on the foredecks of the millionaire sailing yachts anchored for the summer in its ample harbor.

Below decks, similar bodies, stripped of their bikinis, and wearing nothing but flip flops strain against cabin ceilings, humping desperately to the strains of Jimmy Buffett, emanating across the water from island bars running at full blast. *"Come Monday—I've got my hiking shoes on—"* "Tried to amend my carnivorous habits...but at night I'd have these wonderful dreams, Some kind of sensuous treat—Big warm bun and a huge hunk of meat—Cheeseburger in Paradise!"

All this, while tourist families bike out to the Commodore Perry monument, a huge shaft reaching skyward from the center of the island, like a phallus, to memorialize Commodore Perry's victory over the British in the Battle of Lake Erie during the War of 1812. "We have met the enemy and they are ours."

It was Friday and Put-In-Bay was already heating up for the weekend. Families were travelling on the ferry, trying to keep their children away from the floating population of women chasers and drunks who emigrated there every weekend. When we reached Put-In-Bay harbor, we transferred to "Poosie," the 39-foot Sea Ray Sundance, Brucie kept at anchor there. His captain, a six foot vixen wearing yellow rubber sea boots, with leotards up to just under her breasts, and nothing but a fishing vest on top, ran us the rest of the way across the lake to North Bass, jabbering over the ship to shore radio with other boaters all the way. Around her lithe waist, she wore a gun belt holstering a Glock 9-millimeter and, laying on the helm in front of her, were three extended magazine clips containing thirty three bullets a piece. Her name was Ludmilla. The lake was rough today, and pretty soon I grew silent and turned green as the huge Sundance pitched and yawed, attacking the four footers at 30 miles per hour.

Finally, it happened. Like a serpent slowly weaving out of a basket, my lunch crossed my epiglottis on its way back up, triggering my gag reflex, and I bolted for the side of the boat, exploded into the water, and watched my spew drift away in a sickly, but relieved, trance. The boat was crewed by two people, one of whom spent all of her time carefully massaging Brucie's stricken groin as we made the crossing, "to keep him from getting sea sick," while watching me toss my cookies. She came over and put her hand on my back as I sagged over the sidewall, praying to die and watching fish surfacing to eat my puke, and she said, "That's alright. I was gonna do you next."

"I look forward to these little runs on the Poosie," Brucie said, when I regained my composure. "They're always stimulating, and so relaxing." I glanced down at the sad state of his frail sacroiliac in his wrinkled Lido tank suit. *That Gallipolis farmer's buckshot had taken all the gayness out of being gay for Brucie,* I thought to myself. Then, I thought about Rosanne for a minute.

Two men with Chinese assault rifles slung over their shoulders and a bullhorn hailed us from the North Bass dock as we approached. There was a 20-foot rubber patrol craft tied up to the dock, with a 250 horsepower Yamaha Four-Stroke bolted to its wooden transom.

"Putting in on North Bass?" one of them yelled.

"We brought Soft Craw with us," the vixen yelled back.

"Ok, bring him on in."

"It's our little code," Brucie explained. "Helps keep unwanted visitors out. I'm Soft Craw. That's what they call me." The vixen reversed engines and heaved to, as the dock men caught the Sea Ray's lines. In another minute, she and her crew hand were helping Brucie out of the boat, leaving me on my own to hoist my 300 pounds of heft up over the rail to the dock by myself. Everybody seemed to be ministering to Brucie, but for some reason, Ludmilla managed to whip out a camera and snap a picture of me disembarking.

"Just for security," she explained. "We photograph everyone who disembarks at this island—not that many do. For the most part, our security turns away any boater who comes into our quarter of a mile perimeter. But you're the boss's guest."

The place looked a little like an armed camp. The entire shoreline was covered with dense trees, preventing any view of the island's interior from the lake. About 100 feet back from the docks, an obviously new nine foot stockade fence ran in both directions for as far as I could see, separating the dock and shoreline from the rest of the island. Its wide gates lay open, with a Hummer, painted in green and brown camouflage paint, straddling the entrance. More guards with more Chinese assault rifles stood around it. In fact, the place was crawling with armed men, mostly tall thin and black. Many were wearing colorful skullcaps and looked to be foreign. Just inside the stockade was a landing strip.

"What are you planning to do with this island, Brucie?" I huffed, trying to catch my breath, but glad to finally be back on solid ground. "Turn it into some kind of nuclear armaments plant?"

"I've already done what I planned to do. C'mon, let's go in and you'll see." He walked me to the Hummer and issued orders to take us to the lodge. The gates closed behind us, and the Hummer began moving down a single-lane road, like a squat armored beetle, through a cornfield, toward a plain-looking white clapboard farm house. Doubling as "the lodge," the edifice was the largest of ten houses on the island, now all vacant. "Robert picked this house to be his little fishing get-a-way the one time he was here to look over our new venture, so we call it The Lodge," Brucie explained.

I was surprised. "Robert Steinglass?" I asked. I couldn't imagine Bob as a fisherman, much less a partner in a venture with Brucie.

"That's right. As I told you, Bobbi was my partner in this little venture...silent partner."

An extremely cut, completely bald man with eyebrows like Sean Connery's, in his late 50's, wearing nothing but black Lido bathing trunks, tight as a string around his small well-worked-out hips, and earrings with matching nipple rings, answered the door. "Hey, Brucie," he rasped without excitement. Obviously, this hulk spent the better part of his day working out, and looked so strong, he had muscles in his face.

"Meet Winston Barchrist," Brucie announced. "He's my lawyer. Winston, this is Harold. He's the care-taker."

Flexing his well-defined chest, Harold reached across to shake my flabby hand, which he duly crushed in his, like a vice. Looking my body up and down through his pronounced steely eyes, with a tinge of disgust, he growled, "Hello." My hand started turning blue. "You wanna Red Bull or somethin'? I got Four Loco too."

"No, I'm fine—thanks."

Clearly, "the lodge" was more than just a little fishing getaway. Stepping inside, I noticed all its windows were covered with decorator fabric blinds in dark purple; its walls were draped with heavy red satin curtains down to the floor, which was of black marble composite; and, there was a white bear rug in the middle of the floor. A massive fireplace, done in Petoskey Stone, commanded the room, with a gold framed oil copy of Botticelli's *Birth of Venus* centered over it, and tiny inset spotlights illuminating it from the ceiling. A mirrored credenza dominated another wall, with a built-in bar behind it in a wall alcove, containing glass shelves and vodka bottles. The place smelled a little like burnt lawn clippings. On a step-up, into what once may have been the dining room, a Bow-flex dominated what was obviously now a weight room. I could imagine the vixen from the boat and Harold rolling around, grunting and screaming in this place, more than I could picture Robert sitting here picking over his fishing lures.

"Nice decorating," I told Brucie. "So you bought North Bass Island to turn it into a bordello?"

"No, more like a plantation," he replied, laughing. Strangely, as we were talking, Harold picked up a camera and photographed me too, as I stood in the middle of the lodge.

"Harold, do you have time to drive us out to the vineyard?"

Harold looked disappointedly at the Bow-Flex. Obviously, this was going to cut into the five hours of work-out time he'd planned for the day, but Brucie was the boss.

"When?" he grunted.

"Now," Brucie ordered.

The four-wheel-drive pick-up bounced along the lawn surrounding the lodge and out into the rolling fields beyond. There was no road to the vineyard. The vineyard was on a gently rolling set of hills in the middle of the island. From it, I could see the entire island with its swath of cornfield completely surrounding us, and beyond that, the stockade fence walling off the whole place from the lake. The vineyard was a curious looking sight, with visqueen propped on stakes, running between each of the grape arbor rows.

Brucie walked over to one of the visqueen tents and lifted it from the corner, high above his head.

"Look in here," he said excitedly. "Just look at all this!"

When I stuck my head under the flap, and knelt down to see what was inside, there were thousands of green slender saw-toothed leafy stars, flat side up, thrusting toward the sun under the visqueen on frail stems. Some of the plants had buds, and there was a green pungent, almost fruity smell—also a faint smell of rutabaga. Quickly, Harold snapped my picture again as I knelt there looking at the plants. I looked at Brucie, who must have known from my face that I was dumbfounded.

"It's all White Widow," he bragged, "marijuana!"

"Brucie, you've got to be crazy!"

"We've also got Black Widow! We grow it here, and cure it in the vacant houses on the island. The rich just get richer," he laughed. "It sells for up to $8,000 a pound. We unload all of it in Canada. That's what helps keep us clear of the DEA. They call it Catawba Cannabis up there. So start boning up on your Canadian law, Winnie, especially their drug laws, since you're gonna be my lawyer again. I just wanted you to see where your fees are going to come from."

"Brucie, I don't want to have anything to do with this. It's illegal as hell! If you weren't a former client, I'd turn you into the cops." The close call I'd had with disbarment in Chicago flashed through my mind.

"Oh, c'mon, Winnie. You're not gonna do that. It's only a little pot." He giggled. "That's the same reaction Robert had when he found out what I was doing."

"But you said Robert was your partner."

"Silent partner—really silent now I guess." He giggled again. "Bobbi didn't know he was getting into the drug business when he offered to help back my purchase of the island."

"But you didn't have anything to do with—"

"Now, now...don't go assuming anything, Winnie. To assume makes an ass out of 'you' and 'me.' No, I didn't have anything to do with Robert's death."

I passed the Marion Correctional Institution on my way home from the lake. It's a stark red brick felon's resort, featuring barbed wire atop 10-foot chain link fences, and quaint watch towers. I cursed the return of my client, Lloyd (Brucie) Bruce, the entire way down route 23. Gefilte fish wasn't enough for him apparently. Noooo! He'd diversified into Loco Weed. And what about my friend Robert? I knew Robert. His reaction upon finding out what Brucie had involved him in would have been swift and proper. Unless there was something I didn't know about their relationship, he would have called the police.

I kept thinking about the movie *Shaw Shank Redemption*. Ohio was so proud of its state reformatories that a postcard collection series had actually been published featuring the older ones, now mostly relics coveted by local historical societies for restoration, like the Mansfield Reformatory, the filming site of the movie I was thinking about.

I wondered whether they incarcerated you at Marion, or in Ohio's premier prison, the Mansfield Reformatory, for drug running. Visions of Brucie and me creeping around one of these barbed-wire enclosures looking for cover from the "general prison population" with sex toughs, weight lifters and drug ruffians chasing us kept popping into my mind. We'd be given 20 years for drug charges. I didn't need that kind of work. RICO violations could be harmful to a lawyer's health.

Chapter Six: Back in Columbus

The Wending Creek Country Club is located on a tract of land that once was the envy of every horse riding enthusiast in Franklin County. Its ninth green is located next to a major horse ford on Alum Creek that was used during the Civil War. Its golf course, designed by Sigmund Ordorff, who put together courses all over the East Coast of the United States during the Gilded Age of Robber Barons, is still the envy of Franklin County's golfers. But time, much to the chagrin of Wending Creek's membership, has not added an elitist patina to the place. Instead, it's now the Jewish Country Club. Known as "the Club" only among its members, the city of Columbus has surrounded and enveloped it to the point that it's presently in a neighborhood where, unfortunately, after you tee off on the fifth hole, a local resident is likely to jump out of the brush while you're looking for your ball, and offer to sell it back to you.

Nonetheless, "the Club" is the chosen meeting place of the Columbus Jewish aristocracy. And this is especially true when it comes to matters of great business import in that community. Thus, I guided my Toyota Avalon down its curvy road to the club house where I was meeting Stanley Meltzer. I hadn't expected an invitation to the Club when Marinda called to make my appointment with him. But Stanley's secretary, who is, of course, trained and paid to the hilt, had asked, "May I tell Mr. Meltzer what this is about?" Apparently, Stanley considered the subject of our meeting to be very important. So he invited me for lunch at "the Club."

I drove up to the front door of the Club, thinking about what Rabbi Billy had said about Abraham, Hagar and Sarah. Maybe the tack I should take with Stanley was that he should do what was right, because he wasn't going to live forever, and he didn't want to be remembered as a bastard who took an inheritance that belonged to someone else and gave it to his Ukrainian wife. Or was that the story of Jacob and Essau? I couldn't remember.

Stanley was a balding man, tall and thin, in his early 60's, with heavy rimmed, almost coke-bottle glasses and a very milky complexion. His hair was still black, his teeth were white and big, and he was dressed impeccably. Yet he slouched, just enough to make himself appear a little gawky. I could feel his black eyes burning through me from behind his heavy lenses.

"Well, Mr. Barchrist," he said. "We meet again."

"I'm surprised you remember me." I countered. "It was five years ago that I was in your office, and we only met for a minute." *Never mind that he thought my name was Barker then,* I thought.

A thin smile creased the lower part of his face. The eyes didn't smile. "Yes, but you don't look much different than you did then. I remember you."

I must have looked down, trying not to linger over the question of what he meant by that, because he said, "Sorry the fates didn't allow us to work together." I didn't say anything. I'd been on Weight Watchers for almost eight months, and I *did* look different—at least a little different.

He put his hand gently on my back, guiding me, and said. "Well, let's go into the dining room and eat." But before I could take two steps, a club member in tennis togs approached us from behind, and greeted him jovially. As Stanley turned to talk to the healthy looking man, I marveled at how out of place this lawyer looked in this club, with his three piece suit and crooked frame, here in the artificial Roman atrium that served as the lobby of a clubby sports activity center. He was only a golfer when business necessitated it, and he didn't play tennis, and I doubt he availed himself of the Olympic-sized pool, with its special lap lanes. Obviously, his only reason for paying the $50,000 initiation and the sizable monthly fee to belong here was so he could mine the place for clients.

"Excuse me for just a second," he said, barely remembering I was his guest. "I'll be right with you." Then he proceeded to converse with the tennis man about the closing on some piece of land off Morse Road. I just stood there for ten minutes, waiting for him to finish. He didn't bother to introduce me.

When we sat down, he handed me the menu and said that the white fish *meuniere* was out of this world. "And, I think you should have one of our Toska Cups for desert."

"What's a Toska Cup?" Of course, I had no idea what white fish *meuniere* was either.

He didn't answer. He was too busy looking past me, scanning the room and waving to various people. He didn't even hear me.

I said a little louder, "What's a Tosca Cup?"

"Oh—it's a honeyed pastry shell with a—"

A woman came over and interrupted, shaking Stanley's hand. He rose awkwardly to greet her and they started talking animatedly about The Columbus Foundation. Again, five minutes of staring around the room for me with nothing to do. Again, he didn't introduce me. I examined the menu to the point where I almost had it memorized.

Finally, the woman left and the waiter came over. "So will it be the white fish and the Tosca Cup?" Stanley asked.

"No, I'd prefer the Vichyssoise and the green salad," I answered. I'd found the Tosca cup description on the menu—crème brûlée in a pastry cup covered with a demi glaze. I could have eaten ten of them without batting eyelash.

Stanley's eyes flashed disappointment as he wrote my order down on his tab for the waiter. "I think I'll have the Steak Tartar. And bring us two Tosca Cups for desert," he said, finishing out his tab and signing it with a flourish. "Well, now we can get down to work, Mr. Barchrist," he announced. "My Secretary said you had some questions."

"Yes, specifically, I wanted to talk to you about Robert Steinglass."

He glanced around the room quickly and whispered, "There is no Robert Steinglass."

"I have reason to believe Mr. Steinglass left his will in the safe at your office."

"Well, he didn't."

"But I have something in writing that says he did." That must have been a little too impudent for the great Stanley Meltzer. A look of scorn slowly enveloped the little black beads behind his coke-bottles.

"I don't know what kind of document you have, Mr. Barchrist, but it must be some sort of mistake." His voice dropped again. "Robert Steinglass is gone, completely. You know what I mean?"

I didn't know what he meant. Stanley Meltzer may have been one of the biggest lawyers in Columbus, but he was also weird. Tony Basheer wasn't the only person who'd told me how quickly he'd erased all traces of Robert from his office. A lot of other people were talking about it, so many that even I'd heard the rumors. The question was why had he done it?

"Well, would you mind having one of your people look again for the will?" I persisted.

"Mr. Barchrist, who is it you represent, if you don't mind my asking? Frankly, I happen to know Robert Steinglass had no close living family, and no descendants." *Well, if that's true, then who were those people I'd seen at Bob's funeral?*, I thought to myself.

"Well, unless he can find Bob's will," I replied, "I guess I'll be representing Anthony Basheer."

"And who might Anthony Basheer be?"

I was shocked that Stanley didn't know about Tony. I also realized this was neither the time nor the place to fill him in. Apparently, he'd even forgotten that Tony had sought to gain entrance to see him in his office.

"Mr. Basheer claims to be Robert's devisee," I declared.

The response caught me off guard. Stanley just exhaled, making a little sound of dismissal. "Hpuh! You've got to be kidding!" He smiled, as if I was some sort of circus clown, play-acting as a lawyer. "I'm not going to get mixed up in anything like this, Mr. Barchrist. If you believe Robert had a will, you know what to do. You're a smart young lawyer. But here's some advice. Be careful."

Previously, that kind of comment would have generated a total loss of confidence in me, but after my recent success in the Ledraque case, I was emboldened. I didn't feel threatened at all. In fact, I felt like trying to take this man, sitting across this well-laid table from me, down a notch or two, by giving *him* something to worry about. It was obvious his secretary had at least reported to him that Tony Basheer was gay when he showed up at the Meltzer Office. I also surmised that, to Stanley, his image as a lawyer in Columbus was everything, especially here in the center of Jewish society—"the Club."

"You knew about Bob's dealings with the Waqf, I presume," I offered casually.

"The Waqf?"

I watched the cautious look entering his eyes, wondering if he was going to pretend he did know, and just dismiss my comment, or whether he was going to say something else, perhaps to get information out of me about this. In any event, I knew I now had the upper hand in this conversation, even if I didn't know where I was going with it.

"A Waqf is an Arab charity, is it not, Mr. Barchrist?"

"That's right."

"Robert Steinglass would not have had any dealings with any Waqf," he said flatly.

Before I could link Tony Basheer's name to my comment about the Waqf, a dark, well-dressed woman in her fifties came up to the table, escorted by a frumpy younger man, and kissed my host's forehead. He smiled up at her sheepishly.

"Stanley, darling—howvar you, my dear? And who might this be sitting at our table today?"

Stanley quickly stood up and pulled a chair out for the woman, perfunctorily giving her a peck on the cheek. "Hello, Zsa Zsa," he swallowed, pushing past the young man as if he didn't exist. Zsa Zsa's companion was short and seemed to have a glazed look of distraction in his eyes, as he pulled out his own chair.

"I'm Stanley's vife," the stylish woman announced, ignoring the kiss. "Ekaterina. It's a Ukrainian name, and this is my son, Boris. Boris heads up nuclear medical research here in town at the famous Arkon Labs. He's studied all over the world. I'm from the Ukraine. You know it?"

I'd heard about Stanley's Ukrainian wife from two sources: Rabbi Billy and Robert himself. She had come to this country at the age of six, Bob used to say, but somehow she never managed to lose her accent. Very headstrong, this busty woman had risen quite high in the world of charitable society in Columbus. She was used to having people take orders from her, including, Stanley, apparently, and she took pains to portray herself as a well-read, well-studied, super intellectual, with a Masters Degree in Eastern European International Relations—almost an advisor to Zbignew Brzezinski—if you believed her. She even claimed to have a close association with a the Ukrainian nationalist group favoring continued close ties to Russia, when the Ukraine separated from the former Soviet Union. But Bob portrayed her more like a female Vlad the Impaler, from the forests of Transylvania—a vampire who'd totally emasculated her son's manhood. "Vat this voman vanted, this voman got," he used to say, mimicking her accent.

"My dear, this is Winston Barchrist," Stanley said. "He's just been telling me that Robert Steinglass was involved with some Waqf."

"Oh, that's ridiculous!" she proclaimed. "Besides, Stanley, dear. Bop's dead. I thought ve could forget about him by now. That's vhat you said, vasn't it?"

More people came over to the table to socialize with the Meltzer's. After another ten minutes of not being spoken to, I got up and said. "I'm afraid I'm going to have to excuse myself, Mr. Meltzer. I have to get back to the office. Thanks for lunch." Then, turning to Zsa Zsa, I nodded and said, "Nice meeting you."

"Who was that?" I heard someone from the group say as I departed. "He was kind of rude, wasn't he?"

I didn't care what those people thought. All I knew was that it was time to get down to the questions of who killed Robert Steinglass and why Robert sent me $5,000,000.

From my car, I called Marinda on the cell.

"Tell me truthfully," I asked. "Do you think I look any different today than I did five years ago when we met?"

"What do you mean?" she asked.

"Well, I mean have I lost any weight at all?"

"Did you take your medicine this morning, boss? You sound a little depressed."

"Never mind, Marinda. Do me a favor and get some probate papers prepared. We need to open an administration of the Estate of Robert Steinglass with Anthony Basheer as administrator. As far as Mr. Basheer's relationship to the deceased goes, put down "spouse." I'll be in the office early tomorrow to read them. Oh, and check the time difference between Paris and Columbus. Tomorrow we'll be making a trans-Atlantic phone call."

"Spouse?"

"Yes, spouse."

Chapter Seven: Learning Arabic

The phone connection crackled incessantly. The call was costing $3.00 a minute. "Ai *Salam Alekim. Awqaf al Noor v' Umma Americi,"* said the voice at the other end. "Yes, can you speak English?" I replied. *"Oui, Monsieur*, just a minute—*merci."* Another voice came on.

"Yes. Hello, what can I do for you?"

"My name is Winston Barchrist," I was shouting—why. I don't know. It just seemed like the right thing to do on a trans-Atlantic call. "I'm calling from America."

"Yes. I can hear you, sir."

"I was given this number to call by a Mr. Robert Steinglass."

"Steinglassa? Steinglassa?" I could hear a muffled conversation in Arabic beginning in the background. "Just a minute, sir, let me check," said the voice in English. Then I began listening to silence, at $3.00 a minute, for a while. Finally, the voice came on again. "There is nothing with a Mr. Steinglassa here."

"Maybe I have the wrong number. Can you tell me where it is I'm calling please?"

"Yes, you are speaking with the *al Noor—Retention for the Extension of the Community in America.* Perhaps you do not have the correct number. There is no knowledge of a Mr. Robert Steinglassa here."

"Well, do you have an office in the United States?"

There was a decisive hang-up at the other end. I knew the language I'd heard initially was Arabic, and I thought the person who first answered had said something that sounded like the word *waqf.* I buzzed Marinda and asked her to get a hold of Tony Basheer for me.

A minute later, she came in. "No number for him they say."

"Call Ballet Met and see if they know how to get in touch with him, Ok?"

She came back again. "He's in a rehearsal. They'll have him call when he gets out."

I turned back to my computer, which was still on the internet, where I'd been Googling the word "waqf" in conjunction with the word "Ohio." Only one item came up, and surprisingly, it had to do with a school just outside of Columbus. I expanded my search to the entire United States. Not that many more popped up. The thing that seemed to stand out about the few entries I could find was that they all were organized as not-for-profit corporations, with no information about their finances or investments, and they were all tied to organizations outside of the United States, like the Kingdom of Saudi Arabia—Ministry of Higher Education, the Hamdard Laboratories of Pakistan, the Province of Allahbad in India or the Supreme Muslim Council of Jerusalem. There seemed to be no purely American organizations among them.

The phone rang. It was Tony.

"Do you speak Arabic?" I asked.

"Of course I do, silly," he replied.

"Can you come over to my office? I need your help."

"Just as soon as I can shed my tutu," he kidded. "Don't worry, Winnie, I'll put something else on for you." Gay humor never ceased to amaze me. They were like African-Americans—allowed to speak derogatorily of themselves, among themselves, and they did so, kiddingly, all the time, but nobody else was permitted to say anything about them like they said about themselves.

I was going to have Tony call the people in Paris back for me and talk to them. He would know better how to handle the situation with Arabs than me, and if he knew more about Robert's dealings than he was letting on, he'd be able to use that information without clueing me in, which he didn't seem to want to do. My only other option was to cash the $5,000,000 money order; do nothing; and wait for somebody to surface and ask me why I hadn't earned the money. I preferred to have Tony intercede, especially since I wasn't an Arabic speaker, and I'd heard it was a language where a lot could be lost in the translation.

While I was waiting for him, I decided to call Rosanne and pick her brain for a while. She was not only my girl but she was a CPA, and she helped me with accounting problems when I encountered them in my practice, which wasn't very often. You didn't need to know how to read a balance sheet to handle a DUI or a PI case. I wanted her to explain to me how to put a value on a law partnership interest when a partner had died. My guess was Stanley Meltzer's partnership agreement with Robert was silent on that issue, as he had only allowed three of the people who worked for him to be in some form of partnership with him. If I was going to be representing Tony Basheer now in an action to unwind the partnership in order to get him his inheritance, much as I hated the thought of doing it, I would need any knowledge Rosanne could impart to me on this subject. Basically, I didn't see any way to ask Tony for his help with this waqf thing if I didn't take his case on, and I'd rather represent him than Brucie.

"Hi Winston." Rosanne always sounded perky on the phone. "What's up?"

"I've got a hypothetical for you," I began. "It involves a triangle. There's this lawyer who died, and his wife stands to inherit a partnership interest he has, but it looks like there's going to have to be a partnership dissolution to do it."

"You're so cryptic, Winston. I didn't know Robert Steinglass was married."

"Very few people did."

"Well. Who was he married to?"

"Oh—someone who's with Ballet Met."

You're kidding—a ballerina?"

"Well, not exactly."

"Winston, you're so foxy and sly. C'mon. Tell me. Who's the other partner? What kind of business was Bob in? I thought all he did was practice law?"

"That *is* all he did."

"Oh my God!" she replied. "The other partner's Stanley Meltzer?"

"Right."

"Haven't you heard Winston? Stanley Meltzer's in the hospital. They're saying he had a massive heart attack."

"You're kidding. I just had lunch with him yesterday. Who's they?"

"Who's saying he had a massive heart attack? I'm Jewish, Winston. I get stuff like this through the Bexley rumor mill where news travels fast."

Bexley was a Jewish neighborhood and also the venue of Rosanne's office.

"How bad was it?" I asked.

"That, I don't know. I'm surprised you haven't heard anything from Bob's wife since you're representing her."

"Him," I said.

"Him?"

"Never mind, Rosanne," I evaded. "I'll explain it all when I see you."

Just then, Tony Basheer sashayed into my office. "Gotta go now. Talk to you later."

"What's going on?" Tony asked.

"More than I can handle in one week." I answered. "Stanley Meltzer's in the hospital—heart attack or something."

"Good," Tony replied cheerfully.

"No. Not good," I admonished. "Not if you want what you think is your inheritance."

"What can I do?" Tony asked.

"Right now you can help me. I want you to call that number you gave me and speak to them in Arabic. I want you to tell them who you are and where you come from—you know, the name of your village in Lebanon, and everything. Tell them about your relationship with Robert and that he's dead. Tell them that he died before he could give me the message he was supposed to deliver with the $5,000,000 check. Ask them to find out what I'm supposed to do to earn it, if they don't already know."

"I can't tell them about my relationship with Robert. They're Muslims. It's unacceptable."

"Then tell them you were his male secretary at the law firm and that you knew a little about what he was working on."

"That's a much better idea," he said. "Why didn't you think of that in the first place?"

"Because it didn't occur to me that your relationship with Robert was unacceptable."

"Well, you're not a Muslim," he said.

"Neither are you," I replied.

Marinda put the call through for us. This time we had a better connection. For the next half hour it sounded like an Arab Bazaar in my office. Tony actually seemed to be haggling with them. As the conversation progressed, he tried to keep me posted on what was being said as best he could.

"They know I'm a Christian because my village was in the region run by the Christian Falange Party during the Lebanese Civil War in 1975," he whispered. "I think it's making them uncomfortable." He put his hand over the receiver, while clueing me in. Then, another long exchange in Arabic ensued. After it, he reported, "They don't believe anyone named Steinglass would be involved with a Waqf. *"Nama!"* He seemed to insist into the phone. More Arabic spewed from the other end of the line. "I admitted Robert was Jewish," he told me. "It seems to have fired them up." He pursued the conversation. His Arabic came rapidly and seemed flawless.

"Ah, now we're making progress," he announced. They want to know where Ohio is. I told them it's near Detroit. A long spate of Arabic conversation followed. Then there was silence, while Tony waited. Suddenly, he was just saying, *"Nama, Nama, Nama,"* over and over again. He grabbed a piece of paper and began scribbling something hurriedly in Arabic—right to left, repeating the word *"Nama"* many more times. I looked at him and shrugged.

"What is *Nama?*" I asked.

"It means *yes* in Arabic," he answered. They've given me somebody to contact in Cleveland at either the Dar ul Islam Mosque in Middlesbrough, or the Islamic Center of Cleveland, which is located in Parma, Ohio. His name is Imad al-Din al Katib. He's some sort of religious scholar, and they're telling me all about him.

"Does he speak English?" I asked.

Tony turned back to the phone. *"T'no aleha da'had efu alichnezia?"*

Then back to me. *"Nama*—I mean yes," he said.

"Great! Now finish the conversation and let me debrief you. This little tête-a-tête is costing me three dollars a minute."

It took Tony fifteen more minutes to finish the conversation, but finally I heard him say, *"Inshallah,"* and he hung up.

"What was that all about?" I demanded. "Do you realize how much day-time trans-Atlantic conversations cost?"

"Winston, Arabs just don't hang up on each other when they're through talking. It's not polite. They were asking me all about my family and I asked about theirs. They invited me to come to Paris and see them, and to stay in one of their homes."

"I thought they didn't trust you because of all your village's Falangist dealings. They were enemies of the Muslims in Lebanon. I remember."

"Ah, that was at the beginning of the conversation Winston, but this was the ending. We are now friends."

"What is *Inshallah?"*

"It means God willing. It's what I told them when they said I should come to Paris to see them."

"Tell me what you learned about this Imad...al...whatever."

"Imad al-Din al-Katib? He's a big scholar in this country—not an Imam, but a very learned man. He's a representative of King Faisal of Saudi Arabia's education ministry to all the Arab university students in Ohio, Michigan and Pennsylvania."

"Why do the students need that?"

"Who knows? You'll have to ask him."

I called Marinda into my office and asked her to phone both the Dar ul Islam Mosque in Middlesbrough, and the Islamic Center of Cleveland to see if she could find Imad al-Din al-Katib. "When you find him, ask when I can get an appointment to see him," I told her.

"Will do, Mr. Barchrist," she said. "What shall I tell Mr. Katz you want to see him about if they ask?"

"Katib, not Katz, Marinda. Tell them it's about Robert Steinglass and that $5,000,000 money order. Oh, and get me whatever you can off the internet on the Dar ul Islam Mosque and the Islamic Center of Cleveland."

Chapter Eight: Learning Ukrainian

When I got back to my apartment that night, a phone message was waiting on my answering machine. It was from Ekaterina Meltzer. "I vant to meet you at your office tomorrow," she said, in a thick Slavic accent.

That was impossible, I thought, even though I wanted to accommodate her. I just couldn't picture a woman like Ekaterina Meltzer, bedecked in the heavy jewelry and make up, and the designer clothing she wore, sitting in my musty office over a Dairy Mart Store on one of the more sketchy streets in German Village. I called her back and suggested the Claremont as a meeting place instead.

"No, darling, that vill be impossible," she replied. "It's much too early for me to be seen in public. You know my Stanley just died don't you?

"Well, I'd heard he was sick...but..."

"Vell, now, he's dead," she said, in a very matter-of- fact tone. "It vas his heart."

"I'm so sorry," I offered. I was flabbergasted—first Robert, and now Stanley Meltzer!

"Vell, don't vorry about it. If you don't vant to meet at your office, then come to my house tomorrow. It's a day before the funeral but it vill seem alright to everybody. I vill make you launch. You do eat launch don't you?"

"Yes, I do. I'll be there." There was a click as she hung up without saying good-bye.

I lay down on my couch, waiting for tomorrow to arrive, and flipped on a Cincinnati Reds baseball game.

I didn't care much about the Reds as a team, probably because of their colorful past. Marge Schott, their former owner, liked to smoke at the games, even though the Reds played in a non-smoking stadium, and she was well known for her slurs against Blacks, Jews, Japanese people and homosexuals, and her statements in support of Nazi party leader Adolph Hitler. When she died, a huge sigh of relief emanated from the team throughout Cincinnati. Pete Rose, the Red's famous switch hitter, was accused of gambling on the games while he played in them, and he was denied induction into baseball's Hall of Fame because of it. Both these baseball giants were born in Cincinnati. It must have been something in the water there. Today, the Reds were losing again. I thought about calling Rosanne to find out if I should take anything with me to Ekaterina Meltzer's tomorrow, but instead I fell asleep and slept through the night and into the next morning until it was time for me to go see Ekaterina Meltzer.

The Meltzers lived in an English Cotswold Cottage style home on North Columbia in Bexley, Columbus's oldest suburb. "Cottage" is a bit of an understatement actually. The home was an 8000-square-foot stone mini-mansion in a bucolic setting set far back from the street. The maid let me in.

"Vat I vant to know, is vhat you know about the Vaqf," Ekaterina said confidently, sitting down on the couch across from me in her sumptuous living room and crossing her bare legs prominently. The woman was wearing stiletto heels.

Fairly seductive, even at 55, she didn't exhibit any signs of being a bereaved widow. A light turtle-neck with heavy gold jewelry tightly wrapped just under her chin covered any signs of sagging in her neck, and her dark brown eyes pierced through me like TV security cameras from underneath the ample shock of black hair set in bangs over her forehead. She'd obviously had some work done on those eyes. She looked like a well-dressed gypsy.

I stared at her blankly. Why would she ask a question like that? I remembered Stanley saying something about the Waqf when I first met her at Wending Creek. She seemed to know what a Waqf was then, but she'd just blown off my suggestion that Robert had had any dealings with the waqf at the time.

"Absolutely nothing," I replied. "Until recently, I didn't even know what a waqf was."

"And, vhat caused you to learn, darling? That's vhat I vant to know."

"One of my clients," I offered.

"Vhich one of your clients, darling? This is vhat I'm asking you!"

If this succubus wanted to know that, there could be no good reason why, I thought. "Sorry, that's privileged information," I replied.

"But, darling, I don't see vhy. I need to know this, or I vouldn't be asking. You can understand that, I hope." She leaned forward over her bare crossed knee, touching my arm with a manicured hand that had a ring on every finger.

"Attorney-client privilege," I responded, shaking my head no and withdrawing. *If she wanted this information, let her get it by reading her tarot cards*, I thought.

"How can I make you understand?" she inquired, faking that she was hurt by my rejection.

"I guess my question is why do you want this information from me?" Oddly, she was really seductive, but I continued to hold out.

"Before Stanley died," she began, dropping her accent, "he discovered that Robert Steinglass was accepting money from some overseas vaqf, in the

Middle East, through the law firm's account, for reasons unknown. He suspected Steinglass of linkage to domestic terrorism forces in this country at work on various university campuses. As you may or may not know, Stanley and I have been fairly prominent in the Columbus Jewish Community, and in the National Jewish Community, even to the point where Stanley was a past president of the International Student Organization—Hillel. It wouldn't look very good to have his partner linked with this sort of thing, would it?"

"So that's why everything concerning Robert Steinglass disappeared from Stanley's office so abruptly, as soon as Bob died, right?"

She remained silent. Then she changed the subject, turning her accent back on. "I also vant to know vhy you were meeting with my husband that day at the club."

"Sorry, attorney-client privilege again," I replied.

A sneer creased her dark face. "Same client, I suppose," she retorted cracking an ironic smile.

This time, I remained silent. Dropping her veneer of pleasantness, anger welled in her eyes, and her lips became tight and thin.

"It's that male *shiksa* Robert was partnering with, isn't it, or should I say *shagitz*? Vhat's his name—Tony Basheer, or something?" Her voice was raised, and she was clearly more than merely disgusted.

"What's a *shagitz*?

"It's a non-Jewish boy, darling," she said, fighting to recover her dignity.

"You mean like me?"

The anger flashed again.

"Vell, I'll tell you right now," she continued, ignoring my question, "I never liked Robert from the beginning, and vhen I found out he vas gay, I tried and tried to get Stanley to let him go because I felt he couldn't be trusted. But Stanley insisted he vas brilliant. Then vhen he started his secret dealings with that waqf of his, vell, darling, it made me so mad I told Stanley to do anything necessary to get rid of him. It made me so mad. It vas also going to spoil our reputation in the community!"

I got up with great difficulty from her deep couch, and announced, "I think, I'd better be going."

"Not yet," she ordered. Then her tone changed. "Please, I promised you launch, and you haven't had it yet." She rang a little bell on the tea table between the two couches, and the maid brought in a very Mediterranean lunch of dolmades, pita bread, cucumber salad, chick peas, dates and figs. I snarfed it all down, intending to leave quickly, but the maid then brought in wine and lemon cakes, which I couldn't resist.

"More launch?" Ekaterina said seductively. This time I succumbed—to more lunch, that is—and snarfed down seconds on everything. I was still hungry, but I forced myself to get up.

"Ve must keep in touch, Mr. Barchrist," she announced, pointedly, as I departed. "Something tells me ve vill, because I know my guess that Mr. Basheer is your client is correct. She raised her voice but kept her smile. "I've read all the papers in that little estate administration you filed in the probate court for Robert's estate. Really, darling, do you think that's going to enhance your reputation as a lawyer? I mean, really—with Anthony Basheer as the administrator because he's Robert's 'spouse'? See you in court as they say."

I called Marinda on my cell as soon as I got to my car, just to check in with her before heading downtown. She said there were two things waiting for me.

"First, the office of Imad al-Din al-Katib (she murdered the pronunciation) up in Parma, at the Islamic Center of Cleveland, returned your call. They want you to come there right away," she said. "They can see you tonight, and they won't talk to you over the phone—only in person, and only in the mosque."

"And, secondly?" I asked.

"A package came for you from Lloyd Bruce, marked top priority."

"Did you open it?"

"No."

"Well, don't. For all I know, that idiot has sent us a bomb! I'm going to Cleveland tonight, but I'll be in to see that package before I go." I was joking about the bomb, but Marinda didn't see it that way.

When I got to the office, the Columbus bomb squad was already present. Apparently, she was trying to show me she could take the initiative. Officer Shapiro was there too, since my office was on his beat.

"All I can say, counselor, is you're gonna' owe the CDP a lot of money if there's no bomb inside that thing," he announced. Do you have any idea what it costs every time we have to roll out the Ordinance Disposal Unit? That cardboard box doesn't look any too dangerous to me."

It wasn't. The inside of the box turned out to contain documents concerning a construction contract for a marijuana bakery Brucie was planning on building on the island, and a box of chocolate covered dates. He knew I couldn't resist them from the old days when we'd worked together.

"Well, counselor, ain't that too bad—no bomb, just candy. You're gonna get a pretty big bill for this."

Marinda started crying. I hated it when she did that.

"Ok, Jerry," I replied, knowing he didn't know what he was talking about. "Just send me the bill. Right now I've got to get on the road to Cleveland."

"What's up there?" he asked.

"The Cuyahoga River," I shot back, facetiously. Jerry was the nosiest cop in the Columbus Police Department.

"Oh, and Marinda, write Lloyd Bruce a letter and tell him that I can't represent him on this bakery project of his. Just say I've declined the engagement. You can sign my name."

I grabbed the box of dates and left. I figured the drive would take two and a half hours.

Chapter Nine: Cleveland

I think there were 24 dates in that box from Brucie. I must have finished three quarters of them on my drive up to the City on the Lake, because when I reached the Islamic Center of Cleveland, for the first time all day, I wasn't hungry. The ICC was a real experience.

The building was massive. Built in the Moorish style of architecture, it was white with stripes of red brick running through its walls at intervals, and two beautiful domes of gold leaf with tall minarets on each side. The mosque was in the shape of an octagon with white pillars inside, rising from a floor bathed in Persian rugs. The rugs were dotted with bent over men here and there, rocking back and forth and murmuring as their foreheads touched the floor.

I arrived at the time of the Asr, or fourth ritual prayer session of the day, but unfortunately not in time to hear the beautiful calls to prayer of the Muezzin. The mosque had been in existence, as both an Islamic Center and a mosque, since 1967, and Saudi Arabia's King Khalid had paid off the mortgage on its predecessor building. But Marinda's brief internet investigation of the new Islamic Center of Cleveland (ICC) revealed that it was nothing like a YMCA, or even a YMCA with a church.

Its former Imam, had been deported in 2007 for ties with three terrorist organizations, discovered when he applied for American citizenship. Before coming to Cleveland, he'd been a recruiter for a bin-Ladin financed precursor to al-Qaeda. His successor was fired for being too moderate, and had been replaced by an Egyptian cleric who could hardly speak English. The Egyptian now teaches fourteen courses at the Islamic University of North America near Dearborn, where the honorary chairman, a Hamas spiritual leader, recently issued a fatwa defending the use of suicide bombings, etc., etc. and etc.

In short, if you can believe what you read on the internet, this was not an organization with which one would expect a Jewish boy like Robert Steinglass to be involved.

Imad al-Din al-Katib greeted me as I tried to remove my shoes, not an easy thing for a 300-pounder to do with no place to sit down, especially one who wears tie shoes like me. He was a kind looking dark man in his fifties, with a goatee, but no mustache, wearing a decorative fez and a grey suit—no long flowing white robe, no keffiyeh, no evident dagger.

"Don't bother with your shoes, Mr. Barchrist," he said. "Let us go outside to talk. It's a pretty day. Don't you think? In fact, let us go to my house, where we can 'grab' some dinner, as you Americans say."

I wasn't hungry, but I said ok. After all, that had never stopped me from eating before.

Once outside the mosque, Imad told me, "You see, Mr. Barchrist, I am not an Imam here. I am (how do you say it?) the 'Scholar in Residence' for religious matters. You must also understand that here at the ICC, there are many different interests existing under the same roof. The Imam is an Egyptian. He is Sunni. We have no Ayatollah, but Iranians are represented on our various committees, as are various other Shiite interests. Then, of course, we must program for those coming from the other nations of Islam who are in the United States in great numbers—the Indonesians, the

Somalis, the Indians, the Turks, the Afghanis, those from Africa, etc.

Did you know, for instance, that there are now over 35,000 Somalis living in your city. Columbus? It's the second largest Somali population in the United States. I don't know much about that though. I am merely the representative of King Faisal of Saudi Arabia's Education Ministry to all the Arab university students in Ohio, Michigan and Pennsylvania. I just have an office here, but no other real function in the ICC."

"Do you teach at the Islamic University of North America in Michigan?" I asked.

"No," he insisted, frowning. "I meant Arab university students at *American* grown state and private universities, not propaganda mills like the IUNA. It's a madrasah of the worst sort in my opinion. But, please, don't ever mention to anyone that I said that. It could be very dangerous for me.

As I explained, here at the ICC we have many different interests under the same roof. Unfortunately, some of them are competing interests, and the IUNA is one that competes with the interests falling under what you might call King Faisal's tent. Shall we say, his Highness is forced to acknowledge Jihadist interests like those of the Islamic University of North America in his reign over the Wahhabis of Saudi Arabia, but these movements are not his "cup of tea," as you might call it. Nor, are they mine. We take a more internationalist point of view."

"What do you consider to be an internationalist point of view?" I asked.

"It is a viewpoint that spreads good public relations between the Ummah and the rest of the world."

"The Ummah?"

"In the context of Islam, the *Ummah* means the community of believers, and, thus, the whole of the Muslim world."

"Tell me, sir, are you in a position to explain why I have received $5,000,000 from the *Banque Postale*?"

He didn't answer.

"Well, tell me something else. Have you ever heard of an organization called Hillel?"

"Oh yes," he replied. "I know quite a bit about Hillel. It's an organization for Jewish university students that started somewhere in your state of Illinois. Today it has over 500 chapters at universities around the world, on every continent."

"And, have you had any involvement with that organization?"

"We do, yes. But that has nothing to do with our meeting. It is not why Robert Steinglass has brought you to us. Why do you ask that question?"

"Mr. al-Katib...."

"Call me Imad."

"Imad, you may not know it, but Robert Steinglass is dead, maybe murdered."

He blanched in horror when I told him this. A look of shock and disgust covered his face. Then he pursed his lips, mumbled something in Arabic and looked away disconsolately.

"What did you say?" I asked.

"*Al-aars*—it means the pimps. Mr. Barchrist, this conversation has made me very worried for you."

"Me?"

"I will tell everything. But first, let us go to my house and eat."

Not surprisingly, I had no trouble eating, even with all the chocolate dates I'd ingested during the trip up to Cleveland. Imad's wife served a delicious meal of lamb mixed with lentils, pita (more pita) and tabouli, with guess what for desert—chocolate covered dates! Or, I should say, her servant, Awale, a thin Somali, served the meal under her supervision. A Black man named Sueliman Marada, from the ICC, joined us for desert.

After dinner, Imad asked what Columbus was like. He'd heard it was a little city, but I explained that it didn't deserve that label because well over a million people live there, making it much larger than Cleveland proper, and everyone who's ever visited says it's a great town.

I was getting tired, but I rolled into my chamber of commerce mode, telling him the United Mine Workers' Union was founded there by John L. Lewis; World War One fighter ace Eddie Rickenbacker was born there; and, the author, O. Henry, wrote from there while he was in the Ohio State Penitentiary. I explained the place had been made even more famous by golfer, Jack Nicklaus; football coaches, Woody Hayes and Paul Brown; and, of course, General Curtis Lemay, to say nothing of Prescott Bush, George's grandfather. Even Beverly D'Angelo, of *National Lampoon's Vacation* series, was born and raised in Columbus.

Imad, of course, had never heard of any of these people, except for George Bush and Beverly D'Angelo of the *National Lampoon's Vacation* series.

"She's that short nice looking blond actress, isn't she?" he offered.

He began telling me about his boyhood in Riyadh; about how beautiful the desert was at night; and, about Mecca and Medina. As he talked, I began feeling woozy.

Sueliman, for some reason, wanted to talk about the population of Somali immigrants, "refugees" he called them, in Columbus.

"Only 10% of them can speak English well enough to get a job," he pointed out. "They're in great need.

They've been coming to Columbus in great numbers to escape the civil war that has been in Somalia since 1986. Somalia is very unstable for them."

Suddenly I was sick. A dull pain that started in my intestines began to spread throughout my body, making me giddy, and I broke a sweat. I'm not sure when I passed out, but I think it was as I was asking Imad why he'd used the Arabic word "pimps" when I told him Robert was dead.

Chapter Ten: The Long Road Back

I woke up in the Cleveland Clinic, not knowing what day it was, or where I was, and I had no memory of how I'd gotten there. A nurse was hovering over me. When I started asking her what I was doing in one of the most famous hospitals in the United States, she simply said the doctor would be in soon to tell me everything I needed to know. Shortly, he came in, holding a work-up of my blood, which he put down long enough to listen to my heart through his stethoscope.

"So, what's going on Doc?" I was trying to act chipper, but I could hardly summon the strength to speak.

He looked at my chart and then up at me. "You're Mr. Barchrist?"

"That's me. Yes."

"Well, in short, Mr. Barchrist, you've been poisoned."

"What? How?" Sleep was overcoming me again, but I tried to carry on the conversation.

"Polonium. It's a very slow acting radio-active isotope. Your size made it even slower, we think. This is an example of one time overeating may have saved a person's life. Your body mass swallowed up the drug, and you eliminated enough of it before it could reach your other systems—liver, kidneys, spleen, etc. We were able to eliminate enough of what remained through Chelation therapy. So you're not going to die. But you will light up Geiger counters for a while.

Ever hear of the Russian federal security agent, Alexander Litvinenko? They think Putin's men killed him with polonium in 2006 in Great Britain. There were also rumors it was to be used on a guy named Victor Yuschenko, the leader of that Orange Revolution over in the Ukraine in 2004. He ran for President in 2005 and won a run-off election with the government-supported candidate. But TCDD, an extremely toxic compound used to produce Agent Orange, was used instead. It didn't work either. It just disfigured him for life. But somehow, somewhere, you ingested a dose of polonium."

A few days later, I was transferred to the Ohio State University Medical Center, where I learned three things: first, that it would take a long time for me to recover completely; secondly, that my health insurer was refusing to cover the situation because my treatment was experimental—only in private corporate America I guess—and, thirdly, that the Cleveland Clinic's bill had been covered by the Saudi Arabian Consulate in Cleveland. King Faisal had had some work done there on his heart not long ago, and I guess he liked it. *Where in my policy did it say experimental treatments weren't covered?*, I wondered.

Rosanne came to visit me every day at the OSU Hospital. She was very worried.

"We've got to find out who fed you polonium," she kept saying. "Who would have access to that stuff? Who would even know it existed? Where did you eat? What did you eat?"

"Dates," I answered groggily.

"What?"

"Dates," I repeated with all the strength I could summon. "I ate lots of dates on the day I got sick."

"Who fed you dates?"

"Everybody!" I was starting to doze in and out again. All I did all day long was sleep.

The only good thing was, I'd lost 25 pounds in the two weeks I'd been in both hospitals. The bad thing was, I was still one very sick puppy. Couldn't keep anything down. Couldn't go to the bath room.

As I slid toward sleep, I dreamed I was developing a new diet that incorporated tiny doses of polonium into a Weight Watchers regimen. Weight Watchers annoyed me—counting up all those points every day. I couldn't afford their pre-prepared convenience meals, like others who actually had them delivered to their doorsteps daily. So, instead, I had contented myself with reading the Weight Watchers' cookbook at bedtime, as I ate my nightly bag of popcorn (sans butter, of course).

What had it gotten me? I now knew that one ounce of flounder contains 23 milligrams of cholesterol, Vitamin A prevents night blindness, zinc aids in the maturation of sex glands and iodine prevents goiters. Oh, I'd been working out too, until they banned me from Life Time Fitness for breaking their Stairmaster the third time. I was certain now that polonium was the answer, at least to my problem. It was just a matter of getting the dosage right.

"Well, let's go over everybody you came in contact with on that day," Rosanne continued, not realizing I was dropping off to sleep fast.

" Trudy Fischel," I mumbled.

"What?"

I was practically asleep now but I could sense my girl friend's annoyance.

"Get Trudy to—"

"Are you having dealings with that woman again?" I remember her practically spitting out the words "that woman!"

Trudy Fischel was my computer resource. Not only was she the best internet searcher I knew, but she could hack into any computer system that existed. I wanted her to research polonium sources in the United States, and maybe get into Imad's computer and the system at the Islamic Center of Cleveland.

Unfortunately, Trudy looked like a slut, and Rosanne hated her. There was no woman on the east side of Columbus who had a worse reputation than Trudy, and there was nobody smarter. It disgusted Rosanne that as a lawyer, I continued to use her on my cases. She thought it was unprofessional. She wasn't wrong. In fact, it was downright illegal, if you're one of those people who believe the Privacy Act is a good law, which I am not. In fact, Trudy had gotten away with knocking off a personal banking machine in New York, but I was one of the few people who knew that. More power to her. I think the Privacy Act is something corporate America just uses to hide its consumer shenanigans behind anyways—like my health insurance company, for instance, with its refusal to cover my current health problem because the treatment was "experimental."

Marinda visited me at the hospital too. At the office, the phone had been curiously quiet...nothing from Imad to find out how I was doing; nothing from Brucie checking on how the construction loan papers for his marijuana bakery were going; and, nothing from Ekaterina Meltzer—alias "the gypsy widow." The only person who'd called was Tony Basheer, to find out if Stanley's estate had been entered on the probate docket yet.

"Marinda, I want you to call Trudy Fischel and get her to come here to the hospital to see me," I said. "Tell her its business, and I need her services."

"Ok, I'll try," she said, "but you know she doesn't get out of bed until 4:00 in the afternoon, and visiting hours here end at 5:00."

"I know. She gets up, and she goes over to Wass's for her *breakfast* sometimes. Have Wass call you when she comes into his bar, and go over there and explain the situation to her. Tell her she's going to have to get up at noon on the day she comes to see me, but it'll be worth her while."

Wass ran my favorite eatery and bar in Columbus. His real name was Herman Wasserberg, and he, like his father before him, had been cooking brats and serving beer on the same corner in downtown Columbus for 50 years.

"Will do, Mr. Barchrist." Marinda only called me Mr. Barchrist when we were planning something and she was excited about the plan.

"Oh, and Marinda—get a hold of Ronny Herimus and tell him I'll be needing his help too."

"Will do, Mr. Barchrist!"

I may have been lying in the hospital feeling lousy, but not too lousy to fight back. First, I had to find out who the enemy was, and then I had to protect myself.

"Also, Marinda, please—check the probate docket to see if the Estate of Stanley Meltzer has been set for first hearing."

"Will do, Mr. Barchrist!"

"And if it has, prepare a lawsuit for the Franklin County Court of Common Pleas against it with the Estate of Robert Steinglass, Anthony Basheer Administrator, as the plaintiff. Allege concealment of assets as the cause of action, and seek the value of Mr. Steinglass's partnership interest as damages."

"Ok, Mr. Barchrist."

"Oh, and Marinda, please watch your typing on that one. I won't be there to proof it."

Trudy and Ronny Herimus came to visit me together at the hospital. Both were aghast when they saw me. I'd lost another 15 pounds and was down to about 260 now.

"Why would anyone do a thing like this to you?" Ron blurted.

"I think he looks sexy," Trudy opined, "even without the hair." I'd temporarily lost most of my hair from the effects of the polonium. But that wouldn't have stopped Trudes from trying to hop straight into my hospital bed with me, had Ronny not been there. The lady harbored a definite crush on me. I know not why. "I like big men," she used to say. That was another reason I think Rosanne hated her. Well, now I was big, but I wasn't really fat anymore, and apparently that was enough to juice Trudy's hormones into high gear.

"Thank you Trudy. Believe me, 'Dr. Barchrist's Polonium Weight Reduction Plan' is something you wouldn't want to wish on your worst enemy—sexy or no sexy."

"What in the Hell is polonium anyways?" Trudy replied.

"That's what I want you to find out for me. I want you to go home and get on your little machine and find out where the stuff comes from and how somebody can get a hold of it. I also want you to break into the computer system of the Islamic Center of Cleveland and see if there's anything pertaining to polonium on their system. Also, please check out the personal PC of Dr. Imad al-Din al-Katib."

A blank look overtook her face, which I recognized very well.

"$500.00," I said.

The look didn't dissipate.

"OK, $850.00, but that's it."

"And what if this stuff's all in Arabic?" she asked.

"Use one of your translation screen programs," I replied.

"I don't have Arabic." .

"Ok, Ok, just buy one and send me the bill. I'll pay for that too."

With that, she smiled.

"And what about me, boss?" Ronny chimed in. "What can I do?"

"You working right now, Ronny?"

"No."

I should have known. Ronny got laid off eventually from every job he'd ever had. It wasn't the quality of his work or his work ethic. It was our wonderful economy. He was one of those millions who just jangled around at the bottom of it, like nuts and bolts in a broken machine, waiting to be cast out when it was time for a recessionary fix.

"Sorry to hear that, Ronny. But I'll pay you $50.00 per day, if you'll do two things for me. Just stay around the hospital here watching who comes into my room and who hangs out around it. Stop anyone who's not a doctor, a nurse or a hospital employee from coming in, and get their name but don't let them in. Come to me first, and tell me who it is, and what they look like. Use your cell phone camera. The other thing is stop every morning at my place; fill up the cat's bowl and change his litter when necessary. It'll be good under-the-table tax income for you."

"Boss, you're always helping me out like this. I just hope I can repay you some day."

"No, Ron. You always earn the money, and I've got a feeling you will this time too."

Ronny was a very special friend. Once, I was sitting at a bar, and a hillbilly walked in with a tattooed floozy and commanded me to move over a seat, "For, mah waf here," he twanged. "She wants a beer, and so do Ah." Both of them were ragged and jumpy, on a cocaine high, or something like it. I guess I didn't move fast enough for him, because he said, "Are you deaf buddy? Ah said slide your fat ass over!"

Two seats down, Ronny moved with alacrity. Moseying over to the guy's barstool with his chest out, he said one word, "Apologize!"

"Wha? You gotta be kiddin,' buddy," came the nonchalant response.

"That was your second mistake, genius," Ronny replied. Then he dumped his beer over the guy's head, lifted him by the throat, crammed him over the bar stool next to me and said, "Didn't you hear him, Win? I think he wants you to move your fat ass over a seat—to this one."

The poor guy, looked up at me snorting with beer in his nose and wheezed, "Naw, please don't do that."

Ever since then, Ronny's been, you might say, my protector, as well as my friend. Whenever he's out of work, I try to find jobs for him to do, and whenever I'm in trouble, I know I can count on him.

"What's going on big guy?" Trudy demanded, touching my arm. "Arabs, polonium, computer hacking—security outside your hospital door—it's like a James Bond movie!"

"I'll let you know when I know, Trudes."

Tony Basheer flounced in just as they were getting ready to leave. "Hi, gang! What's going on in here? Are we having ourselves a little party?" Tony didn't know Trudy or Ronny, but he didn't let that stop him. He took one look at Ronny who was wearing a tank top and shorts and said "OMG...where did you get those muscles?"

Ronny winced and stepped away, rolling his eyes. Trudy just caught my eye and cracked one of her knowing smiles.

"This is Tony Basheer," I said, ah...Robert Steinglass's...ah...widow. Tony, meet Trudy Fischel and Ron Herimus."

"I gotta go," Ronny said abruptly, wheeling around and heading out the door as fast as he could, calling back, "Nicetameetcha," when he was safely away from Tony in the hallway.

Trudy, a much more worldly soul, was more sophisticated in her approach. "I'm so sorry for your loss, Mrs. Steinglass," she offered. "Did you sit *shiva* for him? I should have come. The entire Jewish community heard what happened."

Shiva, I had learned from Rabbi Billy, is a Jewish wake.

"As a matter of fact, I did, but in my own community, honey," Tony snapped back, "and we were all expecting you, but you didn't show up."

Trudy couldn't resist. "Tell me, Winston," she said motioning toward Tony, "in a situation like this does there have to be a will, or can the spouse just take automatically under the Statute of Descent and Distribution, even though—"

"You were asking me about Arabic," I interrupted, trying to deflect the sting of Trudy's comment by changing the subject.

"Tony here speaks Arabic. In fact, Tony is the one who got me involved with the Islamic Center of Cleveland," I explained. Apparently Bob Steinglass was doing some work with them."

"Hmh," Trudy replied. I could see the gears beginning to turn behind her eyes. "Maybe, we should have a look at Steinglass's computer too," she said.

"That will be impossible," Tony blurted. "Stanley Meltzer has removed Robert's office computer to God knows where, and his personal home PC was destroyed at the time of the murder."

"Removed or destroyed?" Trudy interrogated.

"Both," Tony replied, coming close to tears. "His personal PC was smashed, and the police removed the pieces."

Trudy pursed her lips and gave me a knowing look.

"I'll call Jerry Shapiro," I said. "I've got to report what's happened to me to the police anyways—if the hospital hasn't already. But I don't know if I can get him to agree to let you examine the smashed computer."

Chapter Eleven: Eating Chicken Soup But Not Crow

Finally, they let me out of the hospital. Rosanne brought me home and I went straight to bed. She was there beside me when I woke up, waiting with chicken noodle soup. Her nine year old daughter, Gayna, home after school, was there with her. It was so good to see their faces.

"Hello, Pizza Man," Gayna said. That's what her nick-name was for me, 'Pizza Man,' because I always brought her pizzas from the best take-outs in town. "Looks like you haven't been eating your pizza," she said lovingly. I was down to 250 pounds now but I wasn't hungry. I told Rosanne I didn't think I could eat the soup.

"Winston, did you take your pills this morning? Are you getting depressed?" Rosanne worried. "Maybe you should call Arnold Goldstein."

"I don't need to talk to that talking head."

"He's a psychologist, Winston, not a talking head. He just sees his patients over SKYPE. Remember? That's what you wanted, when you started with him because it costs less."

"Well, I'm not depressed."

"I don't know, my dear. You're something, and it's not yourself. You're not eating. If you get any thinner, pretty soon the Trudy Fischels of the world will have you in their clutches."

"Rosanne! It's just business with her."

"She left a message on your phone—something about the Islamic Center of Cleveland's computer," Rosanne reported. "I didn't understand it all, but she said there were lists of different student groups on different college campuses and code names for each group, with schedules of meetings with Hamas representatives, and there was something about the Somalis working here in Columbus at the Shackman's Distribution Center. I don't know. You'll have to listen to it yourself. I didn't know the Shackman's had Somalis working for them. Do they work in their furniture stores and the department stores too? I shop at Shackman's sometimes but I don't think I've ever seen any Somalis there. Of course, they're a huge business. What's it all about, Winston?"

"I don't know Rosanne. I'll have to listen to the message later. I'm pretty tired right now."

"Maybe we should just go then, my dear—leave you alone for awhile."

"Ok, but please don't despair. There's nothing with Trudy. She's just working for me. I'm taking my medicine, and I'm not depressed. Ok? Please?"

When they left, I dozed off with my cat, Sachmo, sleeping on me. I had heard Shackman's hired a lot of Somalis but I didn't know anything about it. About an hour later, Sachmo flew off my chest in response to a loud knock at the door. Outside in the hallway stood Harold, the workout freak from North Bass Island, and Brucie's power boat vixen, Ludmilla.

"Not expecting, us, huh?" Harold rasped

Ludmilla barged in without being invited, and began looking around, as if she was searching for weapons, opening drawers and such, and checking out the closets. Harold stayed in the doorway, blocking any chance for me to exit.

"What's this all about?" I demanded. I was light headed.

"Don't get your water boiling, honey," Ludmilla snickered. "We're just making sure you're cool before we take you to see Brucie."

"Brucie! Where's he?"

"On the island," Harold growled.

"On North Bass Island? I'm not going up there with you."

"Wanna bet?" Harold answered, leering at me.

"Look, I just got out of the hospital, and besides, I don't want anything to do with that place. I don't want to go there again—ever!"

"Awe?!" said Ludmilla, feigning sympathy for me. "C'mon, you'll enjoy the trip." She took me by the arm, sensually, but I quickly pulled away and sat down heavily on the couch, making it evident I intended to use whatever weight I had left to blunt any attempt to get me out of my apartment and down the stairs.

"Look, I told you, I just got out of the hospital," I said.

"That why you haven't performed on any of the work Brucie sent you over two weeks ago?" Harold growled.

"Feel the inside of my thigh," Ludmilla invited. "Go ahead. Feel under there." She lifted her skirt slightly and put my hand up it. "I don't think you want to make me use that," she warned. "Do you?" She was referring to the six-shot Colt snub nosed revolver I could feel strapped to her strong thigh as I reached toward her crotch.

"Even your thighs couldn't possibly attract me back to North Bass Island," I said insolently, and with that, Harold cracked me across the face with the back of his hand.

"Harold, don't!" Ludmilla ordered. "Remember what Soft Craw said. Any problems, and we're supposed to call him. I think we've got a problem."

You bet you do, I thought. *There's no way the two of you are going to force a man who weighs what I do to do anything—Colt snub nose or not.* Of course I'd forgotten I didn't weigh that much anymore.

"Would you mind if I used your phone?" Harold asked politely.

"Go ahead. Be my guest," I condescended.

When he finally got through to Brucie, he handed the phone to me, as I sat on the couch refusing to move. Brucie explained he'd sent the two of them down to Columbus "to fetch" me because he needed to talk to me right away about a big deal he had in mind.

"Didn't you get my letter?" I asked. "I can't represent you. I don't want to be involved in your operations on North Bass Island."

"Oh, don't be foolish, Winnie," he replied. "That's just simply not an option. You're already involved. You're my lawyer."

"Well, I hereby resign. I don't want to be involved in anything that you're doing. You're involved in illegal activities. Gefilte fish wasn't enough for you. Now, you've sent two thugs down here to force me into your drug business. Frankly Brucie, you've gotten pretty mean, ever since that Gallipolis farmer shot up your groin."

"Wait a minute. Calm down, big boy," he said. "Maybe right now my business has to be kept quiet. But that won't always be the case. Ever hear of medical marijuana? It's legal in Montana and 14 other states, including the District of Columbia. Right now, the stuff has to be grown indoors in most cases, in tiny businesses that use a lot of electricity to light and heat the stuff on a 24-7 basis. But I plan to corner this market with my North Bass Island operation. If left alone, I can produce enough stuff out-of-doors in the spring and summers to supply the whole medical marijuana industry's needs for a year."

"You said you were selling what you grew in Canada," I reminded him.

"Yah, but that's just for now, until we get on our feet, and until the medical laws settle a little bit more in the United States. We're also selling to mainstream bakeries that are contracting for pot-laced pastries. That's where you come in. I need a lawyer. We're gonna build an industrial-sized bakery on the island. By the way, where's my contract? How's it coming along?"

"Your contract never made it out of the blocks! I'm not working on it, and I'm not coming up there to see you."

"Fine. Have it your way! No contact with me if you don't want any. Stay down there. But you're gonna be my lawyer, or I'm gonna screw your moose."

"And just how do you plan on doing that Brucie?" I asked brazenly. Actually, I was pretty terrified by the whole interruption he'd perpetrated on my recovery, but I guess after surviving a poisoning, there was really nothing left to fear. I'd just go to the police.

"What's your little girl friend's name? Rosanne, or something like that? Do you think she'd like a visit from Harold? Oh, and don't bother going to the police. What do you think all the photographs we took of you on the island were for, your scrap book? The newspapers will get a nice story if I go down. So remember big buddy—attorney-client privilege." His voice trailed off into high pitched giggles. "Don't violate it! Hey, speaking of *mousse*, you remember that big *paté* deal of mine that fell through? Don't let yourself wind up like I did." Now he was laughing hysterically. "So where should I send my fee checks big guy? Is your office still in the same place, above that little convenience store? Now, put Harold on the phone please," he continued dismissively.

Harold grunted a few things into the phone. Then, he hung up and he and the vixen left.

My God! He threatened Rosanne! Rosanne had a daughter who depended on her as a single parent. Ok, so I wouldn't call the police about Brucie just yet, but I still wasn't going to do any of his legal work. I hauled myself up off the couch. It was time to get back in the saddle again, even though I still felt too lousy to go downtown to the office. I reached for the phone and dialed Trudy Fischel.

"The ICC's server was filled with files containing lists of what seemed to be meetings between Hamas representatives and campus student groups," she reported. "Everywhere—Ohio State, Ohio U, Kenyon College, University of Toledo, Wayne State in Detroit, Michigan State in Lansing, Pitt over in Pittsburgh, Penn State, etc."

"Middle Eastern students or American students?" I asked.

"I couldn't tell. Mostly it was like the students had been assigned numbers and their names weren't being used, just addresses, which seemed to be their home town addresses or something. I don't know. The few names that did appear, and there weren't very many, seemed to be both Middle Eastern and American."

"Did you see the name Robert Steinglass anywhere?"

"Yes."

"And?"

"And, nothing! There was just a file entitled Robert Steinglass. He wasn't among the lists I'm telling you about. I couldn't get into that file."

"Did you find anything about polonium in their files?

"There was only one thing: an article from the *Cleveland Plain Dealer* about the death of some Russian guy named Alexander Litvinenko. It was emailed to somebody named Dalmar Abdikarim in Yemen."

"Wait a minute. Let me write that down. Ok. What about Imad al-Din al-Katib's PC? Did you get into it"

"Couldn't find it, but there was lots of stuff on him on the ICC's server. You know it's all in Arabic, and so that takes a little time to figure out what's being said. By the way, thanks for the new Arabic Language Translation Screening Program. I'll send you the bill."

"What was on the server about Imad?"

"A lot of communiqués from the Ministry of Education in Saudi Arabia—something about a project for teaching English to Somalis, and some other matter I couldn't make out. I don't know, it all seemed a little crazy to me, but they think they're going to improve Islam's image in America by teaching English to Somalis. I don't get it. Somalis are Africans aren't they? What have they got to do with Saudi Arabia?

"They're also Muslims."

"Oh, and here's something strange. One of the communiqués even mentioned Josh Shackman here in Columbus—you know the guy who runs Shackman's Department Stores and all of the other Shackman interests. There a very big family."

"What about the Shackmans? What did the communiqué say?"

"Nothing really. I just remember seeing the name. It surprised me."

"Trudy, keep trying to find Imad al-Din al-Katib's PC on the net, and get into it. I remember him mentioning something about Somalis here in Columbus."

"Um, I don't know."

"Look Trudy, I'll pay you a thousand more if you keep looking."

"Well, ok, but only if you let me come over and look in on you. I'd like another gander at that new svelte torso of yours."

"That's fine, Trudy, but call first, Ok?"

"Why? So you can make sure your little friend Rosanne's not around? I know she hates me."

"No," I lied. "So I can make sure I'm dressed first."

"Awe, that's no fun," she teased.

When Trudy hung up, I immediately dialed Billy Goldman. Billy was fast becoming more than just my rabbi. He was virtually my guide to the Columbus Jewish community, and the Shackmans were Jewish.

"What do I know about the Shackmans?" he said. "They're without a doubt the biggest Jewish family in Columbus—not only in numbers, but because they're worth hundreds of millions—not just because of their stores, but in real estate and manufacturing. Some say they're even into the diamond industry."

"Where does Josh Shackman fit in to all of it?" I asked.

"Joshua? People considered Joshua's father, Martin, the leader of the family. When Martin died, Joshua inherited the business. I can't say which parts, because he had sisters who also inherited—but definitely he got the department stores and the furniture business. He's a real mensch—a very fine young Orthodox man. His father was an Orthodox Jew who gave millions to Israel, and toward airlifting the Ethiopian Jews to Jerusalem."

"Are there Somali Jews too, rabbi?"

"No, I don't think so, because Somalia is a Muslim country. Ethiopia is a more tolerant Christian country. If there are Somali Jews, there are very few of them."

"Well, what business would Josh Shackman have then with Somalis?"

"Nothing I know of, except that for some reason he's gone out of his way to hire Somali refugees here in Columbus for his distribution centers. I guess they're cheap labor."

Chapter Twelve: It's Jihad

Ronny refused to drive my car. Instead, he wanted to use his refurbished Bronco truck, which he hardly ever had occasion to take on the open road. I was still too weak to drive, so I acceded to his wishes. Besides, I wanted Ronny along for protection. It was a bumpy ride. We were headed up to Parma, Ohio, to the Islamic Center of Cleveland, and a confrontation with Imad al-Din al-Katib.

Having heard nothing from Imad since my little vacation three weeks ago at the Cleveland Clinic, I was getting very suspicious that he was the one who'd put me there. None of the messages Marinda left for him to call me at home had been returned. It was disconcerting. As far as I knew, he didn't even know if I was alive or dead. Presumably, he'd called 911 when I got sick at his house, but I wasn't even sure of that. His wife and two others were there with him.

These people were murky, and I really preferred not to see them again, or have any dealings with them. But I had to find out why Robert sent me the five million, and there was nobody else to ask. I planned to just walk in unannounced, ask for Imad, and start firing questions at him. If there were problems, Ronny would be there. Being poisoned doesn't give you any incentive to be tactful.

We entered the magnificent building through its beautiful main entrance and walked across the huge empty mosque floor, toward a row of doors at one end.

Maybe they were administrative offices. Or maybe they were just closets. I didn't know.

"Why do we have to take off our shoes, boss?" Ronny protested.

"Because this is a mosque."

"So what? We're not Mohammedans!"

" Don't be such a Redneck, Ron. Do it out of respect for another religion—and they're not called Mohammedans any more. They're Muslims."

"Well, I don't like it all," he protested, removing his biker boots. "These things cost over $300.00. They should at least give you lockers for them somewhere."

We crossed the cavernous mosque prayer floor to the other side, and I knocked on one of the doors. A tall bearded man wearing an ankle length flowing white robe (the Thaub) and a white Keffiyeh stepped out.

"Yes, please?" he said, obviously noting that we weren't Muslims. From beneath his Keffiyeh he shot a cold suspicious glance at Ronny.

"We want to speak with Mr. Imad al-Din al-Katib," I announced.

Without saying anything, the man ducked back inside the door, closing it behind him.

"Nice people," Ronny grunted. We waited.

The door opened again and the same man came out. "*Doctor* Imad al-Din al-Katib is not here," he said.

"Well, where might we find him?"

"I don't know, Sir." the man responded belligerently.

"Well, can we leave a message with somebody?" I figured if I could meet a real person, get his name and office phone number, and leave a written message, I'd have less trouble following up.

"As I told you, Doctor al-Katib is no longer here," the man barked.

"No *longer* here? But I thought he was the representative of King Faisal's Education Ministry—the scholar in residence! You mean he's completely gone!"

"You must make inquire to the Education Ministry of his Highness in Riyadh. I know nothing about it."

"And just how do I do that?"

"I said—it is located in the Kingdom of Saudi Arabia, at Riyadh!" Looking up, the man clapped his hands twice.

I was getting frustrated. "Well, what am I supposed to do? Go to Riyadh?"

"Boss," Ronny interrupted, flicking his eyes to let me know to look behind him.

Four obviously Middle Eastern men wearing jeans and striped short-sleeved t-shirts were closing in on us from behind. From where they had come, I had no idea.

"As-salaam 'alaikum," said the man in white, and he turned to step back through the door in the mosque wall. The men began escorting us out. One of them made the mistake of taking Ronny by the arm, and Ronny jerked away quickly.

"You know what you can do, sonny? You can get my boots for me," he said. The two of them glared at each other. "I'm not gonna be led out of here by any smarmy swammie," Ronny added.

We soon found ourselves standing alone, outside on the mosque's white marble portico. Ron was stumbling to put on his boots. It was almost 7:30 p.m., time for the maghrib—the sixth ritual prayer session of the day—and people were passing by us the other way to go inside. At the base of the marble portico bordering the front arches of the mosque, a Black man knelt, preparatory to prayer, washing his feet at one of the spigots provided there for that purpose. Surreptitiously, he motioned us toward him. When we obliged, he led us around the side of the building to a parking lot. In a car parked at the end of the lot sat Sueliman Marada, the man I had eaten dessert with at Imad's house.

"I saw you enter the mosque," he said quietly. "No doubt you are aware by now that Imad is no longer here. It was too much pressure. They forced the Saudis to recall him to the Kingdom. He left within days of your going into the hospital in Cleveland."

"Who forced them?" My mind was spinning now, too fast to wait for his answer. "Were you there when I passed out at Imad's?"

"Yes, we were very frightened. We thought it was something al-Shabaab had done. We didn't know what happened."

"What's el-shish-kebab?" Ronny piped up.

"Ronny, wait," I insisted. "We'll get to that. But first, I need answers to my questions." Then, turning back to Sueliman, I began cross examining.

"And did either you or Imad go to the hospital with me?"

"No, it would have been too dangerous. I can explain. You see, we—"

I was still standing outside the car, but I reached through the window and grabbed his elbow. He did not pull away, though he looked frightened. He just looked straight at me.

"Sorry to interrupt, Sueliman, but I was poisoned and I almost died at Imad's. I'll be radioactive for the rest of my life. So, before telling me how dangerous things are for you, I need some very specific answers to my questions. Please, just answer my questions first—and then you can explain—Ok?" I felt bad about the rudeness, but the lawyer in me was coming out. I meant to cross examine, and nothing was going to stop me.

"Poisoned—Oh, my God," he said.

Do you know why I received a check for five million dollars?"

"Well, you see, many people—"

"Yes or no, Sueliman!" I tightened my grip on his elbow.

"Yes."

"Do you know where the money came from?"

"Yes."

"Do you know who killed Robert Steinglass?"

"No, not for sure."

"Why was five million dollars sent to me?"

"To establish a blind trust, with you as the trustee for the benefit of the Somali refugees in Columbus, to teach them English, to educate them, to train them in American customs, and mostly, to help end the slave trade in Somali women carried on in the United States from Somalia by agents of al-Shabaab. Al-Shabaab is using its slave trade profits to support their armed insurgency against the government of Somalia. Somali girls in Columbus as young as 14 are being told if they don't follow the pimps, their parents and grandparents back in Mogadishu will be killed."

Much as I wanted to follow up on that right away, I didn't.

"Where did the money come from?" I asked

"From The United Arab Emirates and Saudi Arabia."

"And what did Bob Steinglass have to do with all this?"

"That is complicated, I'm afraid."

"Where do you fit into all this, Sueliman, and how do you know what you are talking about?"

"Another complicated question, I'm afraid."

"Ok," I said. "So now you can say what you want to say. Tell me what's going on in your own words, and make it quick." I got into the car with him while Ronny kept watch outside.

"Mr. Barchrist, do you know what an NGO is?" Then, answering his own question, he continued. "It's a non-governmental organization working with the United Nations. I am on loan to an NGO called the Islamic Relief Organization, which is from Jeddah in Saudi Arabia. My regular job is with another NGO called The International Muslim Women's Union. Its main office is in Khartoum, in the Sudan. Unfortunately, there are no NGOs from Somalia. There is still a third NGO involved here, however, called Human Appeal International, from the United Arab Emirates. That is the one everybody at the Mosque thinks I represent. Its object is to protect rights of Muslims in the West.

You see, these three NGOs have been trying to act together, but for different reasons, to help the Somali refugees in America. The largest refugee group is in Minneapolis and the second largest is in Columbus. I am responsible for aid to the Columbus group."

"And Imad?"

"Dr. al-Katib was the representative of His Highness, King Faisal, who has been very concerned about the image of Islam in the United States ever since 9/11. The King has poured millions into various public relations programs through the Saudi NGO, mostly to establish Middle Eastern studies programs in American universities, but we have succeeded in convincing him that helping Somali refugees in America would do more to advance his desires than any money he spends on public relations through education. Of course, my main purpose is guided by the International Muslim Women's Union, my original employer. The IMWU wants to put an end to slaving in Muslim women around the world."

"That's all well and good, Seuliman, but what about Robert Steinglass?"

"His name was given to us by a Columbus business man."

"Who?"

"A man named Mr. Joshua Shackman, I believe."

"Why?"

"Why, I can't say, except that I know the Saudi's were very uncomfortable about having the Kingdom's name or money associated with anything to do with the Somalis. They wanted to help but with no traceable Arab involvement. The Emirs, with their NGO— Human Appeal International—wanted their contribution spent on bringing slave traders to justice. Mr. Steinglass was an attorney, wasn't he? All I know is what Dr. al-Katib told me, and that was that there would be a blind trust set up through Mr. Steinglass with money to help stop the slaving. And then you showed up instead of Mr. Steinglass. But Imad—Dr. al-Katib—was vouching for you. So I came to meet you for dessert at his house."

I remembered Trudy's references to Robert and to Josh Shackman from breaking into the ICC's server, and I also remembered the waqf Tony Basheer had put me on to in the very beginning—*Awqaf al Noor v' Umma Americi.* "What is *Awqaf al Noor v' Umma Americi*?" I asked.

"I don't know this name. It's a waqf, obviously, but I don't know it."

"How do I know anything you're telling me is the truth? Frankly, I've had a little peek inside the ICC's server, and the names of Robert Steinglass, Joshua Shackman and Dr. Imad al-Din al-Katib all show up there, along with the name of Hamas and many files involving Hamas. Hamas is a terrorist organization!"

"Yes," replied Seuliman, "and regrettably thanks to the efforts of your former president Jimmy Carter, and his Center for Democracy, Hamas is also the elected government in Gaza. There are many organizations enfolded into the Islamic Center of Cleveland, and even not all of them are elected governments like Hamas. I wouldn't be surprised to find groups there supporting Hezbollah, Al Shabaab and even Al-Qaeda. You forget, Hamas started as a charity for the benefit of the Palestinian people."

"And, what is this Al-Shabaab you keep bringing up?"

"Al Shabaab is one of the many violent terrorist organizations in Somalia. Al-Shabaab operates in the southern part of the country. There, it is linked to the now deceased Osama bin Laden and his Al-Qaeda. Here in the United States, it is linked with Somali underworld figures, and it finances itself by trading in Somali slave women through these people. In the United States Al-Shabaab operatives all have the symbol of the crescent moon with a star inside hidden in some way on their bodies so they can identify each other."

"And you say, you thought Al Shabaab was responsible for my getting sick at Imad's? How could that be?"

"Because when Imad told me Mr. Steinglass was killed, I suspected Al-Shabaab immediately, and he told me you had come in Mr. Steinglass' place. The walls of the Islamic Center may be beautiful, but they are very thin, and the tentacles of the Internationalist Jihad reach far. Al Shabaab is the organization that would have had the most interest in blocking our efforts with the Columbus Somali community."

"Ok," I said, "but what makes you think they're the ones responsible for me getting sick at Imad's. They had no idea who I was."

"I don't know."

"And where is Imad now?" I asked.

"I'm sorry, I don't know that either."

Outside, Ronny rapped on the window. "Someone's coming, boss."

"Please," said Seuliman, "Let us both duck down below the windows until they pass!"

We did. He was shaking.

Chapter Thirteen: Little Somalia

Joshua Shackman's office wasn't particularly impressive for a multibillionaire and neither was the man who occupied it. Retiring and overly conscious of his shyness are the best descriptions one could apply to him. That, and—oh yes—very careful, he exuded extreme cautiousness. So much so that I couldn't get in to see him until Rabbi Billy vouched for my bona fides. Yet, unlike other billionaires, this young scion of the Shackman empire went about his way without any noticeable security protection, seemingly unconcerned about his personal safety. What Joshua Shackman wanted to be most careful about was that nobody find out he wasn't the ruthless business man his father had been. Always fearful he'd be swindled by one of the multitude of bankers, investment brokers and venture capitalists constantly pushing deals on him, after the elder Shackman died, he wrapped himself in a coterie of top echelon advisors. Joshua Shackman was unwilling to acknowledge that, although he lacked the steely business tactics of his deceased father, he was far more intelligent.

"He's also much more religious than his father ever was," Rabbi Billy explained, as he examined the photograph-studded walls of Josh's office, all relics of his father's reign. There were pictures of Sidney Shackman in the dig he paid for at the ancient Israeli town of Meggido, photographs of Sidney Shackman opening the Maimonides Institute in Cordoba, Spain, that he funded for study of the great rabbi's Mishnah

Talmud, pictures of him leading United Jewish Appeal Missions at the Wailing Wall in Jerusalem, and there were shots of Sidney Shackman shaking hands with every Ohio Governor since James Rhodes. But there were no photos of Joshua Shackman, other than one of his wife and him with their three children at a local Orthodox Synagogue. Josh was planning on leaving a different legacy. He had built that little synagogue.

Billy Goldman, despite his somewhat speckled past, was one of Josh's closest childhood friends, and that's why Billy was with me today in Josh's office. He opened the conversation when Josh entered the room by introducing me as a lawyer and member of his Sunday study group. Then, he got right to the point.

"I brought Winston here because he thinks you're some sort of an authority on the refugees from Somalia in Columbus," he began.

"Oh yes, I'm aware of you," Josh interrupted, turning to me. "You're a good friend of Rosanne Harmon's, aren't you?"

"You know Rosanne?" I asked.

"Mostly through my wife," he responded. "She's very nice—very bright too."

"Anyways," Billy continued, not particularly attuned to the idea of establishing acquaintanceship by the seeking out of things held in common, "Winston here thinks you can give him some information he's looking for about the refugees from Somalia."

"You want to know about the Somalis?" Josh replied. "Well, then, c'mon out back with me. We'll have to get you a hard hat first."

Shackman's office opened onto a hallway that led back to his main distribution center, a huge automated computerized warehouse filled on one side with goods for his department stores and mail order business, and on the other side, with furniture for his furniture stores.

The place was bustling with motorized mules, highboy lifts and conveyor belts. Dotting the floor, were thin black men, some wearing turbans, and black women moving about in colorful flowing sarongs with scarves hiding their hair. Instead of explaining the operation, Josh first pulled us aside into a carpeted room filled with black children at play, who were dressed similarly to the adults outside. Three white women tended them. One was teaching English to a small group between what looked to be the ages of ten to fifteen. The other two were either supervising the play of younger children, or tending to baby care matters.

"This is the daycare center," Shackman explained. "It doubles as a prayer room six times a day, during the 24 hours the Center's on line. These people are very good workers but very family oriented and they will not leave their children at home to come to work, even with their *lantzmen*. It's worth our while to have this facility because where else am I going to find workers who will work for just above the minimum wage? They speak very little English and nobody else will hire them."

"*Lantzmen?*"

"Fellow Somalis," Billy explained.

"You let them leave work to pray six times a day?" I asked.

"Yes, it only takes about 20 minutes a session, including the wash-ups, and only one of the 8-hour shifts is affected by more than 3 prayer sessions."

"Wash-ups?"

"Yes. Come with me." He led us to a very clean walled off tiled area split by a high wall in the center. The room was huge. On one side were showers and sinks and on the other was a low lying basin with spigots above it. "The women must wash their private parts before praying and the men need to wash their feet," he said. "The restrooms we have for our regular employees just won't do for that. So I had these built."

Suddenly a buzzer went off twice over the PA system, followed by a short foreign sounding chant like noise.

"It's our call to prayer," Josh said. "Now watch this."

Hundreds of black workers in sarongs and turbans began streaming quickly in, washing themselves and heading toward the childcare room. We went back there ourselves, where I could see people lining up on their knees, side by side, and leaning forward to touch their foreheads to what had now become a huge prayer rug. At the front of the room an elderly man called out prayers in Arabic as the congregation knelt forward to the floor repeating them.

"I had no idea all this was going on at your place, Josh," Billy exclaimed.

"Oh, this isn't all of it, Billy. We also provide them, and their children, with one hot meal a day for free in a corner of the cafeteria—Halal certified. For most of them, it's their best meal of the day."

"It must cost you a fortune," Billy pondered. You buy from Halal butchers for them?"

Josh laughed. "Well, I keep kosher and so do they, in their own way. So why shouldn't I do this for them? And it doesn't cost me what you think. Remember these people provide very cheap labor. I just give them these perks instead of what I give to our other employees. They're very poor, but they won't take these jobs without these things, and this is why they come here to work."

"How many Somalis do you have working for you?" I asked.

"At this facility, about 900 plus—company-wide, including Eritreans and Ethiopians, over 2,500."

"Mr. Shackman, do you know anything about Al-Shabaab?"

"*Mamzers!*" he shouted.

"Bastards," Billy translated.

"Al Shabaab is why these mothers won't leave their children at home to come to work here. They're afraid the Al-Shabaab will come to take their daughters away and sell them to pimps in the international slave trade. So I provide daycare."

"And did you know a man named Robert Steinglass?" I continued.

"Yes, he was a friend of my wife's. Did you do any work with him?"

"No, but I may have been about to before he died."

"Let's go back to my office," Shackman said, suddenly. "Now I think I know why you've come here. You're a lawyer and he was a lawyer, right? And, you're wanting to know about the Somalis. Now it's beginning to make sense to me."

Back in the office, Shackman reached into his safe and pulled out a sheaf of letters written in Arabic. Paper-clipped to each one was a typed translation. They were all addressed to Dr. Imad al-Din al-Katib and signed by the Chief Secretary of the Education Ministry in Saudi Arabia.

"These letters contain directives to a Dr. Imad, of the Islamic Center of Cleveland, supposedly from the chambers of the Saudi King himself. They require him to find a lawyer here in Columbus and to put the lawyer in touch with a charity in France called *Awqaf al Noor v' Umma Americi.*

I recognized the name. It was the same charity I'd spoken with over the phone through Tony Basheer, the people who'd given me Imad's name.

"The purpose of the charity," Shackman continued, "was, as I later learned, to promote the interests of the

Arab Community in America as a part of the greater Arab Community of the world. Someone from a Sudanese NGO visited me about this six months ago."

"Would that someone have been a Mr. Sueliman Marada, a black man?" I asked.

"Yes, he said he knew of me because I was the largest employer of Somalis in Ohio. I told him I was Jewish, and although I wished the best for the Arabs in America, I really didn't want to get mixed up with a charity like *Noor v'Umma Americi*, but he told me he hadn't come about the Arabs. It was about Somali refugees in Columbus. Did I care about them? I replied, of course. I have been hiring them for years. And, he said, 'well, for his own reasons, the King of Saudi Arabia cares about them too,' and he added, 'But His Majesty doesn't want to get mixed up with the Somali refugees, just like you don't want to get mixed up with Arab charities."

"Mr. Marada said the Al Shabaab people take these girls and drug them up until they'll do whatever they're told by their masters. Then they make them model in auctions over closed-circuit TV where they're sold around the world for big prices. It's disgusting. Marada said to me, 'You don't want to get involved with an Arab charity? Think about how the King of Saudi Arabia feels about getting involved in something like that.'"

Then Shackman laughed. "Politics! Everybody's got to worry about it for one reason or another."

Billy interrupted. "Well, I can certainly understand the position you took, Josh. You're a pillar in the Jewish Community here, and it wouldn't make you very popular if you got mixed up with an Arab charity, especially when your own kind depend on you so much for their charitable needs."

"Well, I got involved, at least somewhat," Josh replied. I got involved after Mr. Marada explained what was happening in the Somali community here to the young girls with the slaving, and after he told me that the Saudis wanted it stopped because it was continuing to tarnish the image of Islam in America, which was already bad because of 9/11. Marada explained the Saudis couldn't allow themselves to become involved publicly on the side of Somali refugees, let alone try to stop the slave trade, for political reasons in the Arab world. I had seen what these Al-Shabaab hoodlums were doing with my own eyes. They drive cabs here in Columbus to make a living, and they'd come out here at shift change to offer the younger women rides home. If any of them accepted the ride, we never saw them again, and sometimes we saw these men physically force the women into their cabs. I wound up having our plant security people shoe them away whenever they came around. But I couldn't imagine why the Kingdom of Saudi Arabia would want to get into the situation. I made Mr. Marada prove he was being truthful with me before I would do anything. That's how I got these letters. He gave them to me."

"I'm surprised at you for letting yourself go that far in an affair that had nothing to do with you," Rabbi Billy remarked. "The Saudis obviously care only about making Islam look good in this country. They care only about their own interests and keeping us on our oil buying binge. What did you think the people at the United Jewish Appeal would think?"

"Nothing to do with me?" Josh responded. "This was about Somali refugees, not Arabs. Where would I be if nobody had helped my great grandparents when they came here from Eastern Europe? What do you think— they just rode into town with dry goods carts and set up Shackman's Department Stores? No. First they had to work for anybody who would give them a job, like these Somalis are doing, and believe me, the people who employed the earliest Shackmans were not at all like them, and they did it for their own reasons. So what? At least somebody helped us. And, believe me, what the United Jewish Appeal thinks doesn't matter to me. Where do they think they'd be without my contributions?"

Rabbi Billy got a little sheepish looking. I'd never seen him do that before. This Joshua Shackman was apparently stronger than he looked on first impression.

"So do you know what, if anything, Robert Steinglass had to do with all this?" I asked.

"Yes. As it turned out, all the Saudis really wanted was an intermediary to do their bidding for the Somalis, but somebody who would never be suspected of being associated with them, and that person had to have the wherewithal to set up and administer a secret trust here for the use of their money in behalf of the Somalis. So I wound up setting Dr. Imad up with Robert Steinglass, and I just let Bob take it from there. I never saw or heard from Sueleman Marada again."

"Bob Steinglass sent me a money order for five million dollars a day or so before he was killed. Do you have any idea what that was about?

"He sent you that money?"

"Yes, with a note to meet him at the Claremont for an explanation. But he never made it to our meeting. Of course, now we know why."

Shackman's face became ashen. "Well, I don't know the answer to your question for certain but I can make a very good guess. Bob often had dinner in our home. One night he told me that his boss, Stanley Meltzer, had discovered he was doing work for an Arab charity and Meltzer got really mad. The Meltzers are (were) very highly regarded here in the Jewish community for their charitable work, and they were also big supporters of Zionism, mostly because of Stanley's wife. Bob said Stanley was just beside himself when he learned of Bob's connection with the Arabs and that Stanley considered it to have very high potential for embarrassing his law firm and his wife. So he put great pressure on Bob to get rid of the matter. It all happened just as things were coming to a head. Bob had already set up a trust, and he was waiting for the money that was going to be used to fund it. One night he told us he thought he knew just the right person to turn the matter over to—someone who wasn't Jewish whom he trusted greatly. It was probably you. The five million dollars was probably the first installment for the trust fund."

"Me?"

"It must have been you."

"Mr. Shackman, do you think Bob was murdered by Al-Shabaab?"

Shackman turned away and gazed out the window, raising his hands to his sides, waist high with palms up, and he shrugged. The look on his face was pained.

"It's like the Amalekites of old," Billy chimed in with one of his Bible references, "Who for unknown reasons attacked the Israelites in the Sinai from the rear just after the Exodus. Maybe Al-Shabaab attacked Robert Steinglass because he was entering their province."

Chapter Fourteen: Enter the Columbus Police

"Polonium," Officer Shapiro snickered. "Sounds pretty exotic to me. What the hell is it?" We were sitting in the bar at Lindy's, the most upscale restaurant on his beat. Jerry loved to stop in there, ruining the place's German Village ambience whenever he did, with his policeman's togs and black leather sheathed revolver in plain sight. Detective Picard was there too. The Police Department had finally gotten around to asking me some questions about my relationship with Robert Steinglass, because Jerry Shapiro had finally remembered that on the day of Robert's death he'd found me sitting in the Claremont waiting to meet with Robert. That was over a month ago. The wheels of justice turn slowly. In fact, the police were on the verge of closing the matter when Jerry suddenly had his epiphany.

"We really don't have any leads as to how Robert Steinberg died, let alone if it was through natural causes or murder," Picard was saying, "no weapon, no informers, not even anything forensic. His apartment was a mess when he was found, so everybody immediately assumed foul play of some sort, but the family refused to permit an autopsy, so we never knew much more. They wanted him buried right away, and they literally stole the body on the day it happened."

My mind turned immediately to Rabbi Billy's Chevrah Chadisha, but I didn't say anything. Instead, I told them the whole story about the *Awqaf al Noor v' Umma Americi,* Imad al-Din al-Katib, Sueleman

Marada, Al Shabaab and the Somalis. When I finished, I could practically see their brains spinning behind their eyes. Skeptical, Shapiro demanded to know how I knew all this. He didn't want to accept any of it as possibly having anything to do with Robert's death. So I laid the story of my first trip to Cleveland and the polonium on them. Picard was more receptive than Jerry.

"I can see a possible connection between the mess we found at Steinglass's apartment and this Al-Shabaab you're talking about, but I don't see any connection between you and the polonium." He ruminated. "Where would terrorists even get polonium, and why would they choose it as a weapon of attempted murder in your case?"

He's right, I thought, *even though Trudy had discovered some chatter about polonium on the ICC's server.* So I decided to tell them about Brucie's North Bass Island caper and the recent disagreements we'd had over my representing him. I felt bad about disclosing Brucie's business to the police after being taken into his confidence as his presumed lawyer, but Bar Association rules require even a lawyer to report a crime if he knows about it, and growing marijuana is a crime in Ohio. More importantly, somebody had tried to poison me with polonium, and I wanted to know who my enemy was. If it was Lloyd Bruce, I needed to know.

"North Bass Island," Shapiro piped up. "That's out of our jurisdiction!" He was always trying to get out of work, and he always had an answer for everything, even if it was a foolish answer. Jerry wasn't a multi-tasker. Right now he was obsessed with the Steinglass case. He didn't want to consider the attempted murder of me.

"What Officer Shapiro means, I think," Picard interrupted quickly, "is that we're going to contact the

Sandusky County authorities and report everything you just told us to them. I think you should contact them too. Then we can coordinate on this polonium thing."

Shapiro raised the proposition of suicide as the cause. "But why then the mess in his apartment? Somebody could have killed him and then ransacked his apartment," Picard argued. He went on explaining that their investigation had revealed Robert had no reason in the world to take his own life. He was a successful well respected lawyer with a big future in front of him. There were no signs of depression; no connections with the underworld; and, no potential clouds of any type on his horizon. Everybody the police had talked to said he was a happy man. So it was either a natural death or murder.

"Yah, a happy gay man," Shapiro retorted. "Maybe he'd just lost his lover or something."

"Don't you think that's kind of homophobic, Jerry?" I asked. "Besides, I happen to know Robert's lover, and they were very close when he died."

"Still," Shapiro continued with his argument, "at the time he was found, there were no signs of restraint, no signs of struggle. It adds up to suicide, not murder."

"Well, what about the smashed computer in his apartment?" I asked

It was very important to me that the police get to the bottom of Robert's death, because for all I knew, now that I was in his shoes with the money the Waqf had paid me, I could be next. I didn't want his case closed out as a suicide, or death by natural causes, unless they were sure about it. I also didn't want to draw any more attention than was absolutely necessary to the blind trust I was now apparently going to run for the Waqf. And, speaking of that trust, I still needed the trust documents. There were only three possible places from which I could piece them together: 1) the hard drive from Robert's broken computer, now in the possession of the police, 2) Stanley Meltzer's office computer system, or 3) maybe, through Sueleman Marada. I asked what the police had found out about Robert's smashed computer.

"Well, what about it?" Shapiro demanded.

"Maybe it holds a clue to the cause of Robert's death," I offered. "If you guys don't care about it, I'd like to have a friend of mine take a look at it. Maybe something can be retrieved."

"No. No," Shapiro responded. "It's in the police evidence room now, and that's where it has to stay."

"But we'll examine the hard drive," Picard added.

I didn't see any reason to involve Joshua Shackman in the investigation of Robert's death, but there were others to whom I felt the police should talk, and other questions to be asked, besides questions about his work with the Waqf. For instance, why had Stanley Meltzer done away with any evidence that Robert had worked at his office within a day of his death? I remembered how angry that had made Tony Basheer. And, for that matter, why wouldn't Stanley have anything to do with Tony when Tony showed up at his office? Of even more significance, why did Ekaterina Meltzer question me concerning what I knew about the Waqf, after denying resolutely that Robert had anything to do with a Waqf when I was introduced to her at Wending Creek Country Club?

"I think you should talk with Ekaterina Meltzer if you haven't already," I suggested.

"Who's that?" Shapiro asked.

"A vampire," I responded, as I watched Picard noting her name down in his little spiral note book.

"What do you think we should ask her about? Picard queried.

"Ask her what she really thought about Robert," I suggested, "about his way of life, and how she felt it impacted her husband's practice—about how she thought Robert Steinglass might impact her standing in the community."

Shapiro was looking at me like I was crazy. Picard just kept scribbling in his notebook. Then he looked up and said that he'd heard everything I'd told him about Lloyd Brucie Bruce, and he intended to follow up on that first. Suddenly, I remembered the threat Brucie had made about Rosanne. I wasn't about to let her be put in jeopardy just to protect myself. I had to take action to protect her before the police went after Brucie. What if he wasn't the one who'd tried to poison me, but he later found out I'd exposed his operation to the police? Somehow, I had to signal Picard not to contact the Sandusky County Sheriff's Office until I'd made provisions for protecting Rosanne.

"Look, Mr. Picard, as my friend Jerry here has said, that's out of your jurisdiction. Give me some time, and I'll contact the Sheriff's Office up in Sandusky County myself. There may be others who get hurt here besides me."

"Wha?" Jerry exclaimed.

"I hear ya," Antoine Picard said.

When they left, the female owner of Lindy's came over to me to tell me how happy she was that they were gone. "Every time that goddam Jerry Shapiro parks his cruiser outside the front door of my restaurant my business drops by 10%. People just go elsewhere when they see his cruiser parked outside Lindy's with its lights flickering."

Chapter Fifteen: The Fourth of July

Brucie had no intention of leaving me alone. He had his people watching me, everywhere I went, and he had ways of making his presence felt in the most unlikely places—like at the annual Fourth of July Doo Dah Parade. I was down to 230 pounds now, and the Doo Dah parade was one of the few times I was out where the public could see me without having the police nearby. I guess I just wanted to show off my new figure to Rosanne, who was with me at the parade. The annual Doo Dah parade is Columbus' largest gay event.

Once the bane of the city, the Doo-Dah parade had rocketed to its second most popular Fourth of July event in popularity—after Red, White and Boom—an outsized public bacchanal where thousands of sloshed citizens danced and puked along the banks of the Scioto River, while young families watched a half million dollars in city taxes blow up in fireworks, and tried to ignore all the debauchery at river's edge. Parading down Neil Avenue toward the University District, without any solemnity, every local office seeker, even a shade to the left of the of the Tea Party—Republicans and Democrats alike—smiled out of convertibles at potential voters from the raucous Doo-Dah procession as it took over the streets.

Never mind the rainbow of Gay Pride colors carried along just behind the American flag. The publicity is great. Politicians in Columbus used to scorn this event as a procession of debauchery, but that stopped when

Candice Gingrich and Mary Cheney road down the street together a few years ago.

Suddenly, some of the parade participants, known as masked "Fashion Police" broke ranks, zooming over to us on their motor bikes. They said they were going to ticket me at curbside for wearing white tube socks, pulled up all the way from my Nikes to my knees. Then, one of them slipped me an envelope. "Don't open this now," he whispered.

Within seconds, their buzzing Mopeds sped the enforcers away to overtake a gaggle of marchers parading down the middle of the street, dressed as waiters with aprons, and carrying a huge paper-maché image of Mayor Geirhardt on a lettered serving platter reading, "Serve Everyone or Get Served Up Yourself—Bucky!" Whistles and cheers rose up as the ménage of service people passed. The backsides of the waiters were butt naked. They were all men.

Giving in to curiosity, I stepped back from the street and opened the envelope. Inside, there was a note from Brucie and a check. "Your little girl friend looks awful pretty, standing there with you in her shorts," it read. "I want my bakery contract by Monday. Work over the weekend if you have to, and put it in the mail to me. Here's your fee." There was a check for $4000.00 paper-clipped to the note. I hadn't done a thing toward getting that contract ready because I'd vowed to get rid of Brucie as a client. I looked up at Rosanne, cheering and laughing as the parade proceeded by her. Apparently, it wasn't going to be so easy to dump Brucie's legal work. Luckily, Rosanne hadn't noticed me reading the note, or she would have discerned the worried look that was probably claiming my face. She was absorbed in the parade, and enjoying herself immensely.

I put my hand on her shoulder to get her attention. "After this, can we go down to the office for a minute?" I asked.

"Why? You promised we'd have the whole weekend together, remember? No work."

"I just need to pick up something?"

"And what could that be that's important enough to interrupt our holiday weekend?"

I didn't want to tell her it was the paperwork for Lloyd Bruce's bakery construction contract, because I'd made a big deal to her about how I was never going to represent him again. "I need to pick up some paperwork on the trust for the Somalis," I replied timidly. "I have to be at the bank first thing Monday morning with it."

When we got to my office, we found the front door wide open. It had been forced. We took one look inside, and Rosanne yelped, "My God, call the police right away!"

The office was ransacked. All of the desk drawers were open, there were papers everywhere, on the floor, on the table, on the desk—and my filing cabinet had been thrown over. The safe looked ok, but when I checked the bottom-side of my desk top, my double Derringer forty-one-caliber rim fire pistol was gone. Had Brucie's people been here looking for his contract? Had Al-Shabaab paid me an office visit? Rosanne was picking up the phone, probably to call the police.

"Don't touch anything," I told her. "This is a crime scene now."

"I'll use my cell," she said.

Within minutes we heard the siren and saw the cruiser lights. Officer Jerry Shapiro was working his beat today. Naturally, he parked right in front of the Dairy Mart door below us, making it almost impossible for any customers to enter. Slowly, he mounted the stairs and traversed the walkway down to my office, carefully looking from side to side at the scene. He was almost swaggering.

"What's going on?" he asked nonchalantly, leaning against the doorway and looking inside.

"I don't know, Jerry, but we've had a call from the State Lottery Commission about you. They'd like you to move your car downstairs and turn off the running lights. It's interfering with the Dairy Mart's sale of lottery tickets, and the state's in a budget crisis right now you know."

"That's very funny, counselor," he said. "Now how can I help you?"

"Someone broke in, obviously," I said.

"Any suspects, counselor?" he asked. "What about that terrorist organization you were telling us about at Lindy's a while ago?"

"Jerry, come outside with me for a minute." When we were out of Rosanne's earshot, I told him about the note I'd received at the Doo-Dah parade earlier, and how I felt it was a threat to harm Rosanne from Brucie. I explained that Brucie had made a similar threat to cause her harm once before, if I didn't do some legal work for him, and that was why I had asked Detective Picard to hold up on his report to the Sandusky County Sheriff's Office about the operations of Lloyd Bruce on North Bass Island. I wanted to take measures to protect Rosanne.

"What measures?" Shapiro asked.

"What measures?"

"Yah, just what did you think you were going to do?"

"Well, I don't know—for one thing, discuss it with her."

"And have you?"

"No, not yet."

Then, he dropped it on me. A report had gone out to the Sandusky County Sheriff's Office about Lloyd Bruce and his marijuana farm on North Bass Island a week ago. Yes, Picard had held up on sending the report, but only for a week. To his knowledge, as yet no action had been taken against Bruce by the Sheriff's Office, probably because they were coordinating with the State drug enforcement people. It would only take a simple phone call to find out for sure.

"You know, counselor, you're a real drip," he added. "When you work with the police, you tell them everything, not just what you want them to know. It's not like on television. We can't help you unless you help us. And, counselor, you should know by now that when you get into these little capers of yours, you can't do it all yourself."

"I know, I should have told you and Picard that Rosanne had been threatened." I was getting morose.

"Well, all I can say, counselor, is she's an awful nice lady."

Chapter Sixteen: Taking Precautions

The next morning I went to Wass's bar for breakfast. It's my kind of eating joint. You can get four eggs over easy laid out across a big pan of corned beef hash and as many biscuits with honey as you want, all for only $7.99. It's a great place to break a diet, and that's what I was doing. For the first time since being poloniumized, I really felt like eating. For lunch, Wass always had his famous brats and warm German potato salad cooking. I'd be back then too. Watch and weep, Weight Watchers. I'd lost over 70 pounds.

Ron Herimus was there wearing a black muscle t-shirt and a cowboy hat, sitting next to a pretty young thing in a blond pony tail and running shorts.

"Hey, Win. Meet Penelope," he announced. "She's my new running partner."

"Hey Penelope," I answered glumly looking down. She had on those running shoes with the little flashing red lights that kids wear. "Nice shoes."

"Hey," she squeaked back.

"Where'd you guys meet?" I asked, disinterestedly.

"Kroger's, by the deli counter," Penelope squeaked again.

Kroger's was a local supermarket chain. Ronny had perfected his pick-up techniques for women there. He'd hang out, moving from aisle to aisle, looking for a likely score, and then move in and strike up a conversation about prices, or the freshness of the vegetables, while the woman fleetingly admired his muscles. Before Kroger's, he used to hang out in

Christian Science Reading Rooms looking for his prey, but he found it easier to start up conversations in the super market. "You're no good at it," he'd say, "unless you can talk about something you know about. And, the clientele in the reading rooms is way different than what comes into a super market. Everybody's got to shop for food, so the assortment is really a lot more diversified." Ronny seemed to go through women like a hot knife through butter.

"What's a matter, Winnie?" he asked. "Somethin's bothering you. I can tell."

"It's Rosanne," I answered.

"Oh, jeez, Win."

"No, no, it's not what you think. She's in danger. In fact, Ronny, maybe I could use your help."

I explained the situation in detail with Lloyd Brucie Bruce to Ronny, telling him that it was of the utmost importance to me that Rosanne not know what was happening, and that she not feel threatened in the least. We worked out a plan whereby he would never allow her to see him, while never allowing her out of his sight at her home, or at her office when she was there. If she went out, he would follow her. If she stayed in, he'd monitor who entered her house or office. When he slept, he'd have a friend on the stake out. For this, I agreed to pay Ronny $15.00 an hour. If anyone accosted her, he was to intercede. Our arrangement would continue until I called it off, or Brucie was in the custody of the police. I knew this was going to cost me mightily, but it was Rosanne.

"Ok, boss. You got it," he said. "But what's with all the corned beef hash and those biscuits? You look so good now. Don't you wanna keep it that way? Look at all the weight you've lost. I could help you turn what's left into solid muscle if you want."

"That's a good idea, Ronny, maybe later. I think I'm just getting depressed again. Guess that's why all this food's on my plate. As you know, eating makes me happy."

"The proverbial over eater's excuse," Penelope squeaked. "What you need is a good pair of running shoes and a trainer." She crossed her skinny sinewy legs and her shoes beeped on and off at me. "How much did you lose?"

"Over 70 pounds"

"How'd you do that?"

"You don't want to know," I said.

"Meanwhile, boss, what are you gonna do to end all this?" Ronny interrupted.

I didn't know the answer to that, but I knew that finding out who had tried to poison me would go a long way toward finding the answer. No doubt, Brucie was deadly serious, but whether he was serious enough to commit murder was another question, just as whether he was serious enough to actually try to abduct Rosanne was another question. Obviously, I was the one who would have to find this out. The police were hung up on Robert's purported murder, and they'd already handled the Lloyd Bruce matter very clumsily. They weren't going to do much for me unless something happened to justify their efforts.

And on top of everything, I had Tony Basheer's probate matter to attend to. The first hearing was coming up in the concealment action we'd filed against Stanley Meltzer's estate in the Court of Common Pleas. There was a will leaving everything to Ekaterina Meltzer, and Tony's position was that he was entitled to take Robert's portion of the Meltzer law practice against the will. The question was, would the Ukrainian viper show up at the hearing, and if so, would she show up with an attorney?

I had evidence that Robert and Tony were married in San Francisco, and that Robert intended to leave everything he had to Tony, but the value of the evidence depended on whether their marriage would be recognized in Ohio. If the answer was yes, Tony automatically had standing to make his claim against Stanley's estate because, under the Statute of Descent and Distribution, at least half Robert's estate belonged to Tony by law. Otherwise, Tony was dependent completely on the letter Robert had given him a week prior to his death, telling him that Robert's will was in the safe at Stanley Meltzer's office. I had that letter in my possession, but fat chance the will was still in Stanley Meltzer's safe, especially since I'd heard Ekaterina had been hanging around the Meltzer law firm like a vampire searching for blood. That safe should have been sealed at Stanley Meltzer's death, I would argue, but what good my argument would do, I had no idea. Courts, without juries, are little more than the judges sitting on the benches, susceptible to all sorts of influences, including, but not limited to the law.

When I got back to the office, Jerry Shapiro was there. Fortunately he'd parked in back this time. As I walked in, he was trying to come on to Marinda, but without much success. "What do I think about conceal carry?" she was answering him. "I think that if a man wants to carry a gun around with him like an extra little penis, he should have it strapped to his waste like you do Jerry, so everybody can see it."

My timing was perfect, I thought, *but my response to the situation wasn't.* Trying to distract him from the total deflation he was bound to suffer as a result of Marinda's wisecrack, I said, "What's up Jerry?" Marinda tried, but could not prevent a huge raspberry from escaping her lips. Officer Shapiro assumed his official police department mode.

"You ever seen this before, counselor?" He held out a rather heavy looking gold earring loop with a tiny topaz in the bottom.

"No, I can't say I have."

"Our people found it on the floor over the weekend while they were combing for evidence on the break-in you experienced. I just wanted to know if maybe it was Rosanne's. Ms. Weisenheimer here," he said referring to Marinda, "says it's not hers. Any female clients been around lately?"

"No. In fact I haven't had any female clients since the LeDraque case last year."

"Well, who cleans the office?" Shapiro continued. "On the other hand, you don't really have to answer that. Just looking around, I can tell nobody does."

"I do," Marinda said spitefully. "Still."

"Well, I guess that's all I got for now," Shapiro said, wrapping up his investigation. "See ya."

"Wait a minute, Jerry," I said, "not so fast. You're assuming only a woman would wear that. But I happen to know some men who work for Lloyd Bruce who wear earrings." I couldn't remember if the vixen did, but I knew Harold did. "I also wish you'd try to find out if Somali men are in the habit of wearing earrings.

To my surprise, Officer Shapiro actually got out his little notebook and wrote down what I said.

"Lemme know if you think of anyone who wears earrings like this," he said. And then he turned to Marinda. "And you, sweetheart—stay away from any loaded guns, concealed or otherwise." Then he left.

"Asshole," Marinda exhaled under her breath.

Chapter Seventeen: A Day in the Court Room

"You can't find it! What do you mean? It's more than half my case."

"I mean it's not where it should be," Marinda exclaimed.

It was the day of the first pre-trial conference in the action for concealment, filed by the Estate of Robert Steinglass against the Estate of Stanley Meltzer, and we were looking for the letter Robert had written to Tony telling him about the will he'd left in Stanley Meltzer's safe leaving everything to Tony. Without that letter, it would be in the court's discretion as to whether Tony had the authority to prosecute the action under the Statute of Descent and Distribution as Robert's spouse. Ohio does not recognize same sex marriages, and the law under which Robert and Tony had been married in California had been repealed, re-passed, and vetoed by Governor Scwartzenneger. But a California Supreme Court decision had stricken down a State Constitutional ban on same sex marriage. So it was really hard to determine whether their marriage was legal or not in California.

I showed up in Court with Tony Basheer, the "Administrator" of the Steinglass Estate at my side, and Ekaterina Meltzer showed up as the "Executrix" of the Stanley Meltzer Estate with a battery of lawyers and her son Boris following her entourage like a lost sheep. As soon as Judge Combtose asked what the case was all about, we were off to the races. The viper didn't even wait for her lawyers to speak.

"He has no right," she shouted, glaring and pointing at Tony.

Undisturbed by her outburst, Judge Combtose turned to me, waiting for my response.

"Your honor," I began, this is an action by the Estate of Robert Steinglass against the Estate of Stanley Meltzer for the value of Mr. Steinglass's interest in the law partnership between the two men. We—"

"Is there a written partnership agreement?" the judge asked.

"Your honor, we believe there is, but we don't have it. This is also an action for concealment of that document against the Executrix of Stanley Meltzer's estate."

"That's insulting and ridiculous!" Ekaterina barked.

"Well, there's a will leaving this partnership interest to your client I suppose, isn't there?" the judge said, looking at Tony with his pencil at the ready to note down my response.

"That's another problem, your honor. We believe the Meltzer Estate is concealing that will."

Ekaterina Meltzer's battery of lawyers rolled into action. As her lead lawyer spoke up, the young associate at his side produced two law books, firmly placing them on the table with a smirk. From that point on, a second associate pointedly began carefully noting down everything that was said on a yellow legal pad. There was no court transcriptionist in the room.

"Your honor," the Meltzer lawyer began, "without a partnership agreement, Mr. Steinglass had no interest in Mr. Meltzer's estate, and without a will, Mr. Basheer has no provable interest in the estate of Robert Steinglass. We would also ask that the circumstances of Mr. Basheer's administration of such estate be investigated by the Court. He has filed as an Administrator, which means there is no will, not as an

Executor, whose name would be specified *by* a will. That in itself is an admission that there is no will. This is not a matter that should be treated lightly. As you know, Stanley Meltzer was one of the most esteemed members of the Columbus Bar." A vicious smile creased Ekaterina's lips as he spoke.

As she shook her head attesting that everything her lawyer said was correct, her son Boris bahhed something at her side that nobody could understand. Quickly, she silenced him.

It was now time for me to earn my lawyer's fee (or the lack of it, as was the case in this case). "Well, your honor, we believe the partnership agreement and the will are being concealed."

Judge Combtose suddenly exhibited signs of life. "Well, let's assume for a moment that there is a partnership at common law where no written agreement would be needed, but there is no will. If that's the case, what is your client's interest in the Robert Steinglass estate?"

"My client was married to Mr. Steinglass in San Francisco. Therefore, under Ohio's Statute of Descent and Distribution, he has a spousal interest in the estate. The doctrine of full faith and credit demands recognition of the marriage."

The Meltzer lawyer piped up again, as his associate obsequiously placed law books open to specific pages in front of the judge. "The status of same sex marriage in California today is highly in doubt, and of course, here in Ohio, well, folks are a little more realistic than out there. We just don't have it."

Judge Combtose straitened in his chair, leaning over toward me, and shouted, "You've got to be kidding, Mr. Barchrist! This Court has *never* had any interest in making law, and it won't be doing so today. Do you understand me? I won't have this! I'm dismissing this case!"

I could see the eyes of the vampire sitting across the table from me begin to dance. Her son Boris began bahhing something unintelligible again. Oh, what a celebration there would be in Ekaterina's little gypsy camp tonight. Only later did I learn that Judge Combtose and his wife had played a lot of golf at the Wending Creek Country Club with the Meltzer's and he as Stanley's guest.

"Your honor," I entreated, "before you do that, at least let us prove to you that there was a will written by Robert Steinglass."

"And just how do you propose to do that?" the judge snarled.

"There is a letter from Robert Steinglass to my client to that effect."

"Well, where is it?" the judge shouted.

"Unfortunately, misplaced somewhere in my office Judge."

"Well that just confirms everything I've heard about you, Mr. Barchrist. Weren't you in some sort of trouble with the Illinois Bar a few years back? You've got five days to produce this purported letter, and you'd better be willing to submit it to a handwriting expert of Ms. Meltzer's choosing. Otherwise, I'm dismissing this case."

I don't know why, but I walked out of the Judge's chambers with my tail between my legs. Obviously, what had happened to me back in Illinois was still very much on people's minds here in the Columbus law community. Plus, everything I'd done to disabuse people of the reputation a lawyer can get from having a disbarment proceeding brought against him, even where he wins, as I had, was about to go out the window with this case—a gay marriage will contest. I'd be a laughing stock.

"What are we going to do?" Tony asked, as we were leaving. "By the way, did you see the gaudy jewelry that woman was wearing? What a horrible necklace she had on. It was little more than a heavy gold hoop with a little topaz at the bottom—ugly!"

"Leave it to you to notice a thing like that, Tony. Is that all the interest you could muster during the hearing? It wasn't supposed to be a fashion display. It was a First Pre-Trial Conference, and the judge said he's going to dismiss your case."

"Oh, I just thought it was a bunch of legal maneuvers going on. I didn't get that out of it—just a lot of legal mumbo-jumbo to me. But he won't dismiss my case when he sees that letter Robert wrote me. Why didn't you just bring it with us? That was silly."

"No sillier than your being in there daydreaming about Mrs. Meltzer's tastes in jewelry. Weren't you paying any attention? Didn't you hear me say the letter has been misplaced? It's in my office, I know that, but I'm going to have to tear the place apart to find it, and the office has already been ransacked once."

I called Marinda on my cell, and told her that our top priority was finding that letter. I was sure I'd put it in the safe, and the safe hadn't been touched by whoever tore my office apart. But just to make sure, I'd go home to my apartment in Bexley and search for it there too. The thought of Tony's anger if I couldn't find that letter was as disconcerting as the thought of Brucie's anger if he ever found out I'd revealed his little North Bass Island marijuana operation to the police.

Chapter Eighteen: Brucie's Wrath

"She came on to me right out on the street in front of Rosanne's office," Ronny said, "and I thought about going inside to check on Rosanne, but something stopped me."

"Her hard, sexy, athletic look, maybe, huh?" I asked.

"Maybe so, I don't know," he answered. "Why I'm such a sap for the muscular ladies, I'll never know."

"What happened next?"

Ronny's cell phone was close to dying, but he went on with the story. "A minute or so later a bald headed guy wearing earrings pulled around from the back of the office in a black Chrysler with Rosanne in the back seat of the car. The sexy lady grabbed me around the neck, pulled me off my feet, gave me a hard kiss on the lips, and hurled me to the pavement. God she was strong! Then she jumped in the car with them."

His story continued. He ran for his motor cycle and started chasing them. They led him to an undesirable section of Fifth Avenue, where a rib place called Jay-Van's used to be, near a B. & O. Railroad underpass.

"The woman must have been Ludmilla and the man was probably named Harold," I told him. "Did they speak to each other at all?"

Ronny was too excited to hear me. He just went on with his description of the place. Trash covered the ground all round, and weeds sprang from every crack in the huge blocks shoring up the right of way leading to the bridge. The Timken Roller Bearing Plant had been there before, until they tore it down. Now there was just a field with industrial detritus and weeds there. He could see Rosanne sitting in the back seat of the car, her head to one side, a white cloth held over her nose and mouth by the sexy woman, maybe chloroform. There was a windowless tool shed beside the railroad grade. The sexy woman and the bald-headed man struggled to get the dead weight of Rosanne's body inside it.

Parking his bike in the tall grass at the fringe of the property, Ronny began reconnoitering the place. He climbed up the railroad grade, thinking that if he could drop down either beside the shed or through its roof, that would afford him the surprise he needed to overwhelm the two kidnappers. He had his .38 Smith & Wesson Special with him, but he didn't want to use the pistol in a frontal assault.

Suddenly, from above, a small blue helicopter appeared and hovered over the shack. The craft, an MD 500E, landed in the field close to the shack, and the bald-headed man carried Rosanne out over his shoulder and flopped her into the front seat. Then he got into the back, and the copter ascended as quickly as it had arrived, leaving the sexy lady behind.

Ronny pulled his gun and fired at her, and she began sprinting to the black Chrysler. But he turned and shot out two of the car's tires.

"Smart thinking, Ronny," I said.

"Yah, but as I dialed 911 on my cell, she ran for it, and she got away. I thought I'd better stay with the car and wait for the police."

"You did the right thing, Ron," I said when he was finished. "She won't get far on foot. Did you give the police a description?"

"Oh yah," he answered. "You don't forget ladies like that one. I'm just so sorry I failed you boss. They got Rosanne."

I didn't know what to say.

"You did your best, Ron. That's all anyone can do."

I hung up and called the police myself, and asked for Detective Picard. He hadn't yet heard about Ronny's 911 call. The bureaucracy worked slow. I told him I was afraid Brucie's people had abducted Rosanne, but he said although a report concerning the activities of Lloyd Bruce had indeed been made to the Sandusky County Sheriff's Office a few days ago, no action had been taken on it yet. He explained that most likely the Sheriff's Office would coordinate with the Ohio State Drug Task Force on a raid. If there was any evidence of marijuana crossing state lines, the DEA would be brought in. It would take a few weeks to coordinate before anybody could make a move.

"So, Lloyd Bruce would have had no idea the police were wise to him yet," Picard concluded.

Why then was Brucie abducting Rosanne? Because I still hadn't done his legal work on the bakery contracts? Was he really capable of doing such a thing for a reason like that—over not getting his legal work done?

My God! I thought. *Rosanne's daughter Gayna would be home from school in an hour, and looking for her mother, who always left work at 4:00 p.m. so she could be home early for her. Today, I'd have to be there for her instead.* I ran downstairs to the car. How would I explain this to Gayna?

"Pizza Man! What are you doing here?" Gayna asked as she came up the driveway of Rosanne's home.

I didn't want to tell her the bad news about her mother until I knew more from the police. She was a remarkably precocious child who had already suffered a big loss when her mother and father had divorced. I wanted to protect her from suffering more if possible.

"Your Mom's tied up today and she asked me to be here for you when you got home from school. I don't know much about it, but she was called out of town unexpectedly. You may have to sleep at my place tonight."

Gayna stared back at me blankly. "Mom wouldn't leave town without first letting me know that she was going herself, and without letting me know where she was going."

"Well, this time she had to I'm afraid, Gayna." I wasn't lying.

"Where'd she go?"

"I'm not sure, but I think somewhere up in northern Ohio." I wasn't really lying that time either.

"When will she back?"

"I don't know for sure." Still not lying

I watched her bite her lip. Her eyes teared up, and she looked away. "Something's terribly wrong. Isn't it? I want my Mom, Pizza Man," she said, folding herself into me.

"Don't worry Gayna. Everything's alright. She'll be back very soon." *This time, I was lying,* I thought to myself. *It's so hard to lie to a kid.* "C'mon," I said. "Let's go over to my place. I'll take you to Graeter's Ice Cream if you come quietly." She smiled up at me through her almost tears. What was I going to do?

While Gayna was inside Graeter's ordering a double chocolate mint sundae with hot fudge and nuts (for me) and a vanilla cone for herself, I stayed outside and called Detective Picard again. They already had Ludmilla in custody. *Good going, Ronny,* I thought to myself—*pretty smart to shoot the tires out of that car.* Picard told me they were interrogating her as we spoke.

I told him to try to get her to talk about what Brucie was doing on North Bass Island without letting on that the police already knew anything about his operation up there. That way Brucie would think Ludmilla was the one who had tipped the police off to what he was doing, not me. I told Picard that maybe he could trap her into confessing she worked for a guy who ran a marijuana farm by making her think they knew more than they actually knew with little details—for instance that the guy's name who was driving the car was Harold, and that Harold was a work-out freak.

"Oh, and ask her about her boating abilities," I told him. "She operates a boat called Poosie. That will make her think you know more than you know for sure. But don't mention my name."

"OK," Picard said, "but I think our main goal right now is to find out where they've taken your friend, Rosanne Harmon. I don't think we want to lose sight of that."

Graeters was right across the street from my apartment. When Gayna came out with our ice cream, we went up to my place. It was 4:30 p.m. and for all intents and purposes, my work day was over, or so I thought. But when I entered my place, the first thing I noticed was the call light blinking on my answering machine. Gayna flipped on the television. I began checking my calls.

The first caller had a broken voice laden with a heavy accent. The only thing I could make out was that he wanted me to stop something if I wanted things to go right, but that if I continued, responsibility would be placed where it belonged. I didn't understand that message. The second answering machine message was very short, and the voice was clearly Brucie's. "Do those contracts—now! Drop your finished work off at room 802 in the Great Southern Hotel. No police, if you know what's good for her." I understood that message very clearly.

The Great Southern, on the corner of South High and East Main, was Columbus's oldest still standing hotel. Now owned by the Westen, its managers were trying to make a go of the enterprise by also operating the old Great Southern Theatre next door in conjunction with the hotel—offering overnight theatre packages and such.

Much as I didn't want to do any work for Lloyd Bruce, doing those contracts now might be the quickest way to get Rosanne back. Maybe I could get them done tonight, have Marinda type them first thing in the morning, and get them over to the Great Southern by tomorrow afternoon. I should probably coordinate all this with the police, but they worked too slowly, and I wanted Rosanne back a soon as possible.

The last message was from Joshua Shackman. He wanted me to call him. Obviously it was important because when Marinda told him I wasn't in the office, he had called me at home. When I called Shackman back, he told me he had received a very strange message from one of the Somali workers in his plant. The man had said, "If you know Winston Barchrist, tell him he is in great danger." Shackman said the message had come from a newly hired person, named Awale, who had only been on the payroll a week, and that it had been relayed to him through the man's supervisor. He had no other facts and no idea what the message meant.

I hung up and glanced at Gayna, sitting with her little back toward me on the couch, absorbed in a television program.

"C'mon, Gayna, we gotta ago."

"Where to Pizza Man?"

"My office."

"Oh, Pizza man, why? I'd rather just stay here."

"Because I've got some work I've got to do right away that I forgot about. We'll pick it up and I'll do it here at home tonight."

"So why don't you just go down and get it. I can just stay here until you get back?"

"No, you're coming with me."

Chapter Nineteen: Which Cup Is the Pea Under?

White donut powder sprinkled onto Officer Shapiro's lap and across his shirt with each bite, as we sat in an unmarked cruiser on East Main Street watching a plain clothed officer staked out on a bench in a park across the street from the Great Southern Hotel. The plan was for Marinda to enter the hotel carrying a large brown envelope, looking like it contained legal papers, and to leave a note at the desk for Room 802, with instructions to the desk attendant to turn on the message light in the room. In the lobby, Picard, pretending to read a newspaper, would scope out whoever came down to retrieve the message. The message itself said:

> The contracts are ready. To get them, have
> Rosanne present outside the main entrance of
> the Great Southern Theatre behind the hotel at
> noon tomorrow.
> Winston Barchrist III

All night long I had worked up Brucie's legal papers at home in my apartment, as Gayna slept in my bed. Normally, I might have made calls, or even met with the client to determine which way to go in those situations where he had options. But this time I didn't care. I just put everything together for Brucie in the standard manner. I was exhausted. That's probably why I relented in the morning and called the police to let them know what I was doing. I wanted to get Rosanne back as soon as possible, but I wasn't sure they'd just let her go when I came up with the legal work.

The police plan was to offer the documents in trade for Rosanne in broad daylight, with sharp shooters stationed on the roof of the garage across the street from the entrance to the Great Southern Theatre, ready to pick off whoever showed up with her, if necessary. If I saw Rosanne outside the entrance to the building, I was to walk up, hand the documents to whomever was with her, and simply take her hand and walk away with her. Any hesitation and the sharpshooters would fire. I would be wearing a bullet proof vest.

Picard, however, wanted to scope out the hotel and get as much information as he could before we executed the plan. That's what led to the stake out we were now on. Picard wanted some idea of the kind of people we were dealing with. So he called a meeting at the police station for early this morning. There, he briefed everyone, reading to us the reports on Ludmilla's interrogation, which had been completed during the night.

"The bitch never cracked," he complained. "Wouldn't even give us her name, but she fit the description Mr. Barchrist here gave us to a tee—hard body, almost six feet tall, small arm strapped to her inner thigh. All she kept saying was that we were into something far too big for the Columbus Police to handle. 'You'll know that when Al-Shabaab comes knocking at your door,' she warned us. Nobody understood what she was talking about."

"Al-Shabaab—that's the Somali terrorist organization I was telling you about," I reminded him. "Remember?   They're somehow linked with Al-Qaeda?"

"Yah, but that was in connection with the Steinglass case. It didn't have anything to do with Lloyd Brucie Bruce, did it?" Officer Shapiro remarked.

"You say you've had contact with this Al-Shabaab?" Picard asked.

"No, but I know a little about them from my dealings with Robert Steinglass's matters."

Picard calmly made notes about Al-Shabaab in his notebook, as I spoke. Before he closed the meeting he delivered what I considered to be a real bomb.

"Apparently, I told you wrong, Barchrist," he said. "Brucie probably knows we're aware of his marijuana operations on North Bass Island now. The Sandusky County Sheriff's Office reports they discovered he had a mole in their organization—some young deputy, who they've always suspected of being gay. Can't say for sure that he tipped Lloyd off, but it's likely."

"Does that change any of our plans for the swap?" I asked.

"No," he said. "Just be sure to wear that vest we gave you."

Later that morning, Detective Picard emerged from the lobby of the hotel. He got in the cruiser with Shapiro and me and described what he'd seen in the hotel lobby.

"A thin black man came down with a large Caucasian male and called for Marinda's message. There was nothing remarkable about their dress—khaki pants, print shirts with the sleeves rolled up to the elbows. The black man had a very strange tattoo. It was sliced into his arm instead of printed with ink—looked like a half circle with an *x* inside. I approached him and asked for the time. He acted as if he didn't understand, and the white man answered for him. Both looked to be about 45. That's it. That's all I saw."

"Probably a foreigner," Shapiro said, "the black man, I mean."

"Was the white guy bald? Was he wearing earrings of any kind?" I asked.

"No. He looked Middle-Eastern, maybe Hispanic, with lots of dark hair. I'm not sure which."

"Who was the room registered to?" I asked.

"John Smith, not much help there, right? Guess we'll just have to fill in the blanks tomorrow, after we get your lady back."

"Wait a minute," I said. "Did you say the carved tattoo looked like a half circle with an *x*? It could have been the Al-Shabaab symbol—a crescent moon with a star inside. I heard about it once before from a man named Sueliman Marada."

Picard got out his little notebook and started writing again. He wanted to know how to find Marada. I told him to check with the Islamic Center of Cleveland up in Parma.

I had Officer Shapiro drop me back at the office. I'd never worn a bullet-proof vest before. Chances are if Brucie, or anyone who'd known me previously, saw me in it they wouldn't even notice the vest because I'd lost so much weight. I'd heard that even with this type of armor, depending on the caliber of the bullet, I'd be knocked into the dust if I got struck and could be severely injured. I was scared. What if there was a weakness in the vest?

Marinda had unwelcome news for me as I entered the office. "Mrs. Meltzer's on the phone."

The last person I wanted to talk to right now was Ekaterina Meltzer. I was exhausted. The thought of her heavy gypsy-like features flashed in my brain. They revolted me. For no reason, the comment Tony Basheer had made as we were leaving the court house two days before registered in my mind. *'Did you see the gaudy jewelry that woman was wearing? What a horrible necklace she had on. It was little more than a heavy gold hoop with a little topaz at the bottom—ugly!'* Suddenly, it dawned on me that Jerry Shapiro had told me his team recovered an earring like that when the police had combed my office after the recent break-in! Maybe they were a match.

"Yes, Ms. Meltzer, hello?"

"I vas just thinking," she said, "maybe ve could settle our little case. If you vould drop it, I vould be villing to cover your attorneys' fees and expenses."

"I'm not sure I can do that Mrs. Meltzer. By the way, have you discussed this with your lawyer?"

"Oh, no," she answered, "I have discussed it vith the judge himself."

I knew Judge Combtose was tight with the Meltzers, but for her to admit she'd had discussions about her own case outside the ear shot of opposing counsel (*ex parte*, as they say) was beyond propriety. But what good this knowledge would do me was debatable. The judge would deny it. She would deny it. Chances were extremely slim I could get another judge assigned to the case unless Combtose voluntarily recused himself, which he never would. So I decided to take a different tack.

"Tell me, Mrs. Meltzer, do you have a necklace with matching earrings that involves gold hoops with topazes at the bottom?"

"Vhat?" she said.

"You heard me." I knew she would have discovered that one of the earrings was missing by now, if this were true.

Her voice faltered. "I don't know," she said. "I have a lot of jewelry."

"Well, would you mind checking?"

"I certainly vould mind checking, young man. I don't see vhat that's got to do vith anything!" She hung up.

I called the CPD and had them put me through to Jerry Shapiro in his police cruiser. After explaining that Tony Basheer had observed Ekaterina Meltzer wearing a necklace at our court hearing that appeared to be part of a matching set with the earring the police had recovered in my office after the break, I asked him to get a search warrant issued for Mrs. Meltzer's jewelry. "I'm sure Tony can give you any necessary affidavit," I said. "He's got a very keen eye for things like women's jewelry."

"You've got to be kidding," Jerry responded. "Where's the probable cause? We'd be laughed out of court on evidence like that. Plus, I understand Ekaterina Meltzer is very well known and respected. You've got to be kidding."

Chapter Twenty: Shock and Awe

It was noon. A blue MD 500E helicopter swooped down toward the Great Southern Theatre out of nowhere and hovered over the East Main Street entrance. The craft was filled with thin black men, all pointing AK-47 assault rifles at the ground. Police radios crackled. This was not a police helicopter.

A short Mediterranean-looking man in a white long sleeve t-shirt appeared in the entranceway of the Great Southern Theatre with Rosanne handcuffed to his wrist. This was something we hadn't planned on. How could I just go out there with Brucie's legal papers and walk away with Rosanne if she was handcuffed to this man?

So the plan suddenly changed. A police bull-horn blared, "Uncuff the lady!" We all waited, but the Mediterranean man did not follow the instructions. "Uncuff the lady and you will receive your documents!" Still, nothing happened.

"I'm going out there," I said.

"Winston, don't! Not yet!" Jerry Shapiro yelled.

I opened the door of the unmarked cruiser stationed in the entranceway to the parking garage across from the Great Southern; slowly got out and began walking toward the entrance to the theatre with a large brown envelope containing Brucie's legal documents held high above my head in front of me. Each step forward required me to summon the same type of courage that used to propel me off the high diving board when I was a kid. *"Just do it!"* I did it. When I was within 15 feet of Rosanne, the man said, "That's far enough. Just toss the envelope here to me."

"Not on your life," I said. "Let her go first."

A Ruger SR1911 suddenly appeared, and he jammed the barrel to her head. Simultaneously, a zipping sound whizzed by my ear; a red dot appeared on the man's forehead, his hands flew out to the sides, and he fell backward, taking Rosanne down with him. The shot must have come from one of the sharp shooters. Did I hear it? I don't know. All I heard was gunfire erupting from the helicopter and from the top of the garage. Shell casings clinked on the ground and bullet holes climbed almost mechanically up the plaster balustrade framing the stairs of the theatre entrance.

My God! Was Rosanne dead? Everywhere, there were flashes as ordinance discharged. Shots aimed at the police exploded from inside the theatre and from the hotel. Then, just as another helicopter, this time a police helicopter, entered the scene above me, something blew all the air out of my lungs, hurling me to the ground. I was hit! Stunned, I couldn't move.

From the ground, I watched a police officer with an ax running toward Rosanne, who was still fastened to the dead Middle Eastern man sprawled on the sidewalk in front of me. His first blow was to the chain handcuffing Rosanne to the dead man. When that failed, his next blow was to the man's wrist. As he picked up Rosanne and carried her away, I could see the dead man's hand hanging, still cuffed to hers. She wasn't moving. Was she dead? Was she? I tried to get up, but couldn't.

The battle continued from the sky over me until suddenly the tail rotor of the MD 500E burst into flames and ceased spinning. The copter began spinning out of control and fluttered to the ground, hitting the street and scraping around in a circle with a tremendous noise before coming to a halt. As a hissing sound began emanating from the downed machine, it seemed like half the Columbus Police force approached it, crouching behind a fire engine that appeared out of nowhere. Four black men crawled from the wrecked copter and were quickly subdued, but there was no time to channel any water at the burning wreck before it blew up. As for me, I just lay there in the street, watching at pavement level as everything happened around me. Debris from the explosion was falling everywhere. Suddenly, somebody grabbed me by my legs and pulled me out of the street.

"Mr. Barchrist. Mr. Barchrist. Are you alright?" It was Picard.

"Thank God for the vest," I said.

"We got her. We got Rosanne Harmon," he said, "and she's alright."

"Good. That's good," I remember saying. It must have been right after that that I passed out.

Chapter Twenty One: An Unusual Interrogation

The next thing I remember was lying on the gurney in the ambulance. Rosanne was there, but she wasn't being treated. She was just sitting beside me as the truck bumped along, smiling and caressing my hair. I could see welts on her wrist from the cuffs. They must have been put there when the man she was chained to fell backwards yanking her down to the sidewalk with him. That lucky event saved her from the spray of bullets coming from the helicopter above her.

"You saved me," she said, smiling down and peering into my eyes. "You're such a brave man!" She put her hand on my leg as she spoke.

All I could think of was grabbing her, but I was strapped onto the gurney. Instead, I said, "Gayna—I picked up Gayna for you, and she's been sleeping at my apartment."

She leaned over and kissed me. "You're gonna be alright," she said. We just rode the rest of the way to the hospital in silence.

An hour after we got there, Jerry Shapiro excitedly entered the emergency room cubicle where they'd put me, flushed and out of breath like he'd been exercising too hard.

"You look like you've been running from pillar to post, Jerry."

"I have. Things are really happening fast, counselor. I've come to brief you, because I figured you'd want to know right away. You were right! Those men in the helicopter, and at the hotel, they were all Al Shabaab.

Oh, don't look so confused. You were right! It was Lloyd Bruce's organization that abducted Rosanne, but Al-Shabaab and Brucie, as you call him...well they're somehow in league together. They're in cahoots, and we're investigating that right now. We think it's all tied together—the Steinglass murder, Al-Shabaab and Brucie's organization."

"How did you find all this out so fast?" I asked.

"Can you keep a secret? The white man Detective Picard saw in the hotel lobby—the Middle Eastern guy?—he's on Homeland Security's list of wanted people. He's Al Qaeda. We picked him up inside the Great Southern, hiding in the kitchen after the battle. The news stations are already calling it the "Battle of Main and High," and, anyways, the Department used some of its more persuasive interrogation techniques on him."

Any time Jerry Shapiro said, 'can you keep a secret?' you knew it wasn't going to be a secret for long. "Yah, Jerry, you know I always keep your secrets," I said.

"Turns out this Arab's some kind of coordinator between the Lloyd Bruce organization and Al-Shabaab."

"What do you mean persuasive interrogation techniques?"

"The guy's been heavily involved in the illegal trafficking that's been going on involving Somali females in Columbus. He's known and hated by the Somali community here. Picard gave him the choice of the safety of a county jail cell, or just turning him over to them for disposition under their community Sharia Law up there on the North Side. Highly unusual technique, huh?"

"That legal?"

"I don't know. You tell me. You're the lawyer. Anyway, he played the 'Go to Jail' card instead of the 'Allah Akbar' card, and started talking to us."

"So what did you learn?"

"That your client, Lloyd Bruce, is smack in the middle of everything. He's been selling drugs to Al-Shabaab—heavy stuff like heroin. They use it to drug up the girls they abduct before selling them over some kind of closed-circuit TV worldwide auction arrangement. He lets Al-Shabaab operatives from Ohio and Minnesota hide out in a couple of houses he's got on North Bass Island, like safe houses, and he uses them for security on the island. In return for all this, Bruce gets a cut from the slave trade sales."

I don't know how much the police had learned, but this little "unusual" interrogation technique they had used may have put them on to more than they could possibly be expecting. Robert had been Brucie's partner in the North Bass Island real estate deal, a silent partner. That I knew. But he couldn't have known about Brucie's marijuana farm or his drug dealings because he wouldn't have hesitated to turn Brucie over to the police had he known. Did he find out later? Was he murdered because he found out? Did he know about Brucie's connections with Al-Shabaab? How did that connection come about? Had Al-Shabaab linked up with Brucie to get to Robert because of the trust he was going to administer, the purpose of which was to help bring the slave trade to an end? After all, Steinglass's name had appeared on the Islamic Center of Cleveland's server, according to Trudy Fischel. There was a file on him. Why? Who had access to that file? It was time for me to get a hold of Trudy again.

My cell phone rang. It was Gayna, home from school, and at my place, wondering where I was. "I've got a surprise for you," I said. "I'm with your mother right now, and she's coming over to pick you up. Just stay there. The two of you should be together again in about half an hour."

"That's a funny way to put it, Pizza Man."

"Well, I guess I'm just a funny guy."

Rosanne asked me if I was sure, or did I need her to stay at the hospital with me.

"Go," I said. "She needs you more." Actually, I just wanted to call Trudy outside Rosanne's earshot. If she knew I was talking to Trudy, she'd just start broiling unnecessarily.

I made the call immediately after she left.

"Again you're in the hospital?" Trudy said. "What happened this time? You have another polonium flare up? Are the Geiger counters ticking too fast?"

"No," I told her. "You'll be able to read all about it in tomorrow's newspaper. It's too involved for me to go into now. I've got another job for you involving the ICC's server again. I need you to get into that file you found on it involving Robert Steinglass. Is there a way you can tell me who's been accessing it over the past year?" The response was silence. "For, say, $500?" Still silence. "OK, for $1000?"

"For $1000 I'll see what I can do," she said. "It won't be easy. You want me to come over there to the hospital and see you?"

"Nah, that won't be necessary, Trudes. I'm getting out of here in a few hours—I'm sure."

"What are you wearing?" she asked.

"Oh, c'mon! Please! Give me a break." I clicked off.

Chapter Twenty Two: Finally a Break

The morning's *Dispatch* lay on counsel's table in front of me. "PITCHED BATTLE AT HIGH AND MAIN," the banner headline read. A photograph of my body laying in the street amid helicopter parts and other debris covered almost the entire top half of the front page.

As if on cue, Judge Combtose entered the courtroom to the accompaniment of the bailiff's traditional sing-song cry—"All rise." We all stumbled to our feet in the obligatory fashion, leaving me no time to read the article.

"Estate of Robert Steinglass vs. Estate of Stanley Meltzer—case no. 42 CV 1071," the bailiff called.

Ekaterina Meltzer's lawyer rose with pomp to begin, as she sat smiling smugly. "Your Honor, as five days have now elapsed and Mr. Barchrist has yet to produce the letter he claims he has proving that Mr. Steinglass had a will, and that Mr. Basheer is therefore properly before the Court as the administrator (or should I say, administratrix),"—he paused theatrically—"of his estate, we move to dismiss this case with prejudice."

It was true. Not that I wasn't pre-occupied with other matters for the past few days, but Marinda had turned the office upside down and still couldn't find the needed letter. I rose to address the Court. "Your Honor–
–"

"Sit down, Mr. Barchrist. This Court takes judicial notice of the fact that Mr. Barchrist has been otherwise unavoidably occupied for the past few days." With that, he picked up a copy of the *Columbus Dispatch* and dropped it on his desk. "The case is continued for thirty days."

Ekaterina Meltzer stood up and sneered, clearing her throat to speak. Her lawyer pulled her back down. Neither she, nor the lawyer, offered a retort, and we all stood up as the judge proceeded to leave the bench. As everyone began withdrawing, I picked up the *Dispatch* from counsel's table. The story had been sensationalized:

> "It took a kidnapping and the perseverance of a local lawyer wanting to save Rosanne Harmon, his girlfriend, as well as a gun battle between the Columbus Police and a terrorist organization, to uncover a possible connection between Ohio businessman Lloyd Bruce and the Somali group known as al-Shabaab. Police are still investigating the murky details, and it is presently unknown whether Bruce or al-Shabaab abducted Ms. Harmon from her office in Bexley. The reason for the abduction is even more unclear, according to an unnamed police source..."

That unnamed source has got to be Jerry Shapiro, I said to myself. The article summed up where everything stood extremely well. A connection had been established between Brucie and al-Shabaab, but there was still no proof he was behind the abduction.

When I got back to the office, Trudy was there waiting for me. "So, Mr. Hero," she began sarcastically, "Now that you've lost all that weight, I guess you're quite the fearsome guy, at least according to this morning's newspaper. Pretty titillating to be under fire like that, I bet."

"You can skip the humor Trudy," I said. "Have you got something for me already?"

"Yep, I do, boss, Awale."

"What?"

"The only person who accessed Robert Steinglass's file at the ICC was somebody named Awale. He or she's the one who set up the file too. Maybe it's some sort of code name."

"Who's Awale?"

"Pay me another thousand bucks and maybe I can find out for you, boss. Otherwise, knowing the answer to things like that is why you get the big bucks. You figure it out."

I was getting a little sick of Trudy's chiseling. Yes, I decided, I would try to figure it out for myself. I called the ICC in Parma and asked for Awale. Nobody knew who I was talking about.

So I set Marinda to work on the computer looking for the derivation of a name or word like *Awale*. Where did it come from? What nationality was it? It seemed as though I'd heard of it before, but where? In an hour, Marinda came in with results.

"It's a Somali name, boss. *Awale* is a Somali name."

The psychological "aha" response suddenly flashed in my brain. *Awale* was the name of the worker Josh Shackman had warned me about over the phone the night Rosanne was kidnapped—the worker who had said, "If you know Winston Barchrist, tell him he's in great danger." I looked at my watch. It was only 11:00 in the morning. The man might still be at work at Shackman's Distribution Center right now. I called Josh. Awale was still working there and he was there until his shift ended at 2:00.

"Could I come over and talk to him right now?" I asked.

"Yes," Shackman said, adding that he would have his security people hold the man over if I didn't arrive by 2:00. There was no particular reason to rush, but I rushed any way—perhaps more than I should have. I got stopped for speeding.

"We don't normally see too many grey Avalons doing 65 in a 40 mph zone," the cop remarked as I rolled down the window. "It's such a conservative car."

Just give me the ticket and let me go, I thought to myself. *Damn wise-cracking cop. He should only know what I had to go through to move up to this 'conservative' Avalon from riding a Moped around town.* Maybe I could get my friend Jerry Shapiro to make this guy agree in court to drop his citation to an equipment violation so I could just pay the fine with no points.

I would explain to Jerry why I was going so fast to get to Shackman's. After all, Jerry was in on the case. But, then again, knowing Jerry, maybe he wouldn't care.

As they brought Awale in to talk to me at Shackman's, my heart skipped a beat. It was the same man who had been the servant in the home of Dr. Imad al-Din al-Katib the night I had dinner with him in Cleveland. "Who are you?" I demanded. "Are you al-Shabaab?" The man's eyes shifted. He looked toward the door. He was thin and tattered and very scared.

"Call the police!" I told Shackman. He nodded to one of his security people to do so.

"Please, sir, I am just Somali immigrant," the man said.

"Oh, no you're not," I said. "You poisoned me.!"

"No," he insisted.

"Then why did you tell Mr. Shackman here that if he knew me he should tell me I was in great danger? You're with al-Shabaab, aren't you? Aren't you!"

"Al-Shabaab, yes, but no! I not poison you. No, no no!"

"Well, guess what, Mr. Awale? You're going to get the opportunity to explain everything you want to explain to the police. You're going to get the opportunity to explain why there are references to polonium on the ICC's computer. You do, of course, know what the ICC is."

"ICC?"

"You know, the mosque in Cleveland."

" I know nothing of this mosque."

"You did work in the house of Imad al-Din al-Katib. Did you not?"

"Only one night. His wife ask me to help because they having a guest for dinner."

"Oh, save it for the police! I suppose you know nothing of the Waqf set up by Robert Steinglass to help Somali immigrants in Columbus avoid your slave trade either." The man leered at me. "And I suppose you know nothing of Lloyd Bruce!"

"I know not a Lloyd Bruce."

"Winston," Joshua interrupted. "Let the police do all of this. What are you talking about? You were poisoned?"

"Get a Geiger counter and I'll show you!" I admit it. I had lost control of myself. They had murdered my friend Bob Steinglass. They had poisoned me. They had kidnapped my girlfriend. They were trafficking in slave women. I could feel myself shaking with rage.

"Should I call Rabbi Billy?" Shackman asked. "Maybe he can help. You're really beside yourself. Your voice. You're shouting. Calm down, please."

Finally the police showed up and I began explaining the whole story to them. The officers, whom I had never met, looked at me as if I was crazy. I don't know, maybe I looked a little crazy at the time. Awale just sat there looking like a poor disheveled immigrant, and he just kept saying, "No. no no." Finally, when I got to the part about how he had threatened me in my tirade to the police, Joshua Shackman, a man of great esteem in the community, was able to confirm that that was true.

"Ok," one of the officers said, looking at the other. "I think that's aggravated menacing. We can take him in for that."

The other officer looked as if he wasn't sure but nodded his assent anyway, and they handcuffed Awale. I told them that when they got to the city lock-up, they should call Anthony Picard or Jerry Shapiro. One of the policemen didn't bother to wait, and called instead from his radio. I could hear Picard's voice as the officer spoke into a connection on his shoulder, but I couldn't hear what he was saying. Suddenly, the cop turned to me. "You say your name is Winston Barchrist III?"

"Yes, I am."

"Ok," he said to the other officer. "Picard says to bring the man in. He says you can come too Mr. Barchrist, if you want."

Chapter Twenty Three: We Are Still Nowhere

Awale Samatar was in the United States on a refugee visa. A Somali speaker, he was born in Kenya, in an area that had historically been part of Somalia before new political demarcations made his homeland Kenyan. Accused of being an accessory to the 1998 United States Embassy bombing in Nairobi, there were rumors linking him to Fazul Abdullah Mohammed, a Kenyan appointed by the late Osama bin Laden, as Al Qaeda's leader in East Africa. When his denials of these rumors to the Kenyan authorities proved to be of no avail, he fled to Southern Somalia, where he became an operative of al-Shabaab. Known then as *Harakat al-Shabaab al-Mujahideen*, al Shabaab was a youth movement ("the Youth" or "the Lads") fighting to overthrow the government of Somalia and its Ethiopian allies. Captured by the ruling Somali faction in Mogadishu, Awale escaped while awaiting deportation back to Kenya, and with the aid of the U.N. Commission on Refugees wound up flying to New York and entering the United States with refugee status.

Samatar admitted, under heavy police interrogation, being a member of al-Shabaab *in Somalia*, but not in the United States, and he steadfastly insisted that his only role on the night I ate dinner at the home of Imad al-Din al-Katib in Cleveland was as a servant to help Imad's wife. He was trying to earn some extra money by helping her.

As for why he had set up a file entitled Robert Steinglass on the computer of the Islamic Center of Cleveland, he gave no answer, except that he was told to do so. He couldn't remember who told him to do it. He added that he did not consider the ICC to be a mosque, but rather a center for Muslim refugees in this country that provided him with a place to work. He said he came to Columbus because he needed a new job when the period of time he was allowed to work as a refugee at the ICC expired. What motivated him to warn Joshua Shackman that if he knew me, he should tell me that I was in great danger? The answer was truly confounding.

"Because at the dinner in Cleveland I hear Mr. Barchrist ask Mr. Imad al-Din al-Katib why he uses the word *al-aars* (the pimps) when he tells al-Katib Robert Steinglass is dead, and I know, when I hear *al-aars*, this means al-Shabaab. They are selling prostitutes. Very dangerous."

And, why did he feel compelled to warn Joshua Shackman about this?

"Because I hear in the talkings at Katib's dinner that Mr. Barchrist is from Columbus and that he replaces Mr. Steinglass, who was recommended by Mr. Shackman. I worry about this because I know al-Shabaab."

The man was obviously lying. How could he have made any connection between Robert and al Shabaab unless he knew that in Columbus al Shabaab knew that Robert Steinglass was its enemy, and how could he have known this without being in on what al Shabaab was doing in Columbus to the Somali refugees, and what it did to Bob Steinglass? He could easily have been an al-Shabaab spy placed in Imad's home to find out who Robert Steinglass's replacement was going to be.

Be that as it may, there was still no proof as to who poisoned me, who killed Robert, who gave the order to kidnap Rosanne, or why? All we had were artful lies. This man, Awale, could have been the answer to the first two questions, but not the third. Brucie had to be the answer to the third, and it was here that Awale made a mistake. After having told me at Shackman's warehouse, that he didn't know Lloyd Bruce, he admitted to knowing of North Bass Island. When asked how an African refugee might know of such an out-of-the way place, he responded that he once worked there before coming to Columbus. If he worked there, he could only have worked for Brucie.

I called this discrepancy to Detective Picard's attention, and he immediately ended the interrogation without any further questions and called the United States Attorney to ask for assistance from the Feds.

Within two days, the FBI picked up Lloyd Bruce at his home in Fremont, Ohio and began questioning him concerning his relationship with al-Shabaab. They told him immediately that the organization was on the U.S. list of terrorist organizations. A battery of lawyers interceded on Brucie's behalf, but they were unable to prevent real estate records from coming to the fore that revealed North Bass Island had been purchased by a company known as B & R, Inc., in which Brucie owned 60% of the stock, with the other 40% being owned by Robert Steinglass. The Feds did a fly-over of the island immediately, photographing Brucie's marijuana crop with high powered lenses, and that was it. Lloyd Bruce's next stop was the Sandusky County Jail, pending an indictment as soon as a Federal grand jury could be convened. Bail was set at $1,000,000.

He was told things would go easier for him if he cooperated, and if he didn't, an indictment for the murder of Robert Steinglass was in the offing.

Simultaneously, succumbing to "enhanced" or "unusual" interview techniques used by the F.B.I., Awale and some of the other Somalis picked up in the raid on the Southern Hotel and Theatre, admitted to ransacking Robert's apartment, but not to killing him.

Brucie was confronted with this evidence, and he admitted that he and Steinglass had had a falling out over his marijuana business, and that he had sent "his men," the Somalis, down to Robert's to "scare" him and to search his place for documents Robert might have created ratting Brucie out, but he insisted over and over again that "his men" found Robert Steinglass already dead when they got there, and that he had nothing to do with Robert's death. He also continued to maintain the outlandish claim that he did not know "his men" were operatives of al-Shabaab, and that he thought they were merely down and out immigrants in need of work.

"Yes," he said, "I could have been behind the abduction of Rosanne Harmon. I could have done it to scare Winston Barchrist into doing my bidding and to let him know to keep his mouth shut. But I'm not saying I did. So go ahead, indict me for kidnapping, you'll just lose on that one, because you've got no proof. But if you try to indict me for the murder of Robert Steinglass, when it's all over, you'll find your asses in the mother of all lawsuits, because you haven't even got any circumstantial evidence on that one. As for your kind offer that if I cooperate, it will lead to a shorter sentence on the drug charges, my answer to that is—not short enough to see the legalization of medical marijuana. I'd rather be the man who fights for that and then get's rich from it while I watch the many patients who will benefit—God bless America."

Outside the interrogation room in the hallway, Picard asked, "Well, I think we've got that nut on the drug charges for sure, and maybe on kidnapping Rosanne Harmon, but if his so-called "men" didn't kill Steinglass, then how did he die?"

"Nobody is gonna know that until we exhume the body and check it out," the F.B.I. Agent replied. "I can't believe you guys let him be buried without an autopsy. What were you thinking?"

"His family was demanding a quick burial," Officer Shapiro answered. "Something to do with Jewish tradition they said, but frankly I think they were afraid the coroner might find he had aids."

"No, no," Picard argued. "Don't you remember? That big shot boss of his, Meltzer, was pulling strings behind the scenes to get him buried as quickly as possible. It was almost like he wanted him gone and out of the picture. And, it was that high society wife of his that came forward on the family's behalf to insist on an early burial by accusing the police of being callous to Jewish traditions. Nobody in the County Government wanted to tangle with her."

"Well, something just occurred to me," I interrupted. "Before anyone goes and digs Robert up, I think we should try it."

"And what might that be counselor?" Shapiro asked.

Chapter Twenty Four: 450,000 Rads

No grass had yet grown over Robert's grave. Only a pile of freshly mounded dirt lay there in the little part of the cemetery cordoned off for Jewish burials. There would be no headstone in place for a year, and presently, the grave was very simply marked by a small metal marker close to the ground reading "Robert Steinglass." When I pointed it out to Detective Picard and the FBI agent, Officer Shapiro couldn't resist.

"They ought to send you an invoice for all the expenses the department incurred to come up here to Fremont on this little lark of yours if it doesn't pan out, Barchrist."

Ignoring him, Picard motioned to the lab technician in the cruiser to come forward with the Geiger counter. Approaching the grave, the technician turned on the machine with its boom-like wand, sweeping the ground in front of him. At first only a few ticks pocked the silence, but as he continued toward the mound of dirt, they grew steadily in volume and frequency, until the wand was directly over the grave. The machine was now crackling and popping like popcorn that was just about to finish cooking, and the steady sound never faltered.

"Stand back!" The technician yelled, as he read the machine's meter. "I'm getting almost a 1000 mrem."

"What does that mean?" Picard yelled.

Then, the technician dropped the machine and ran back from the grave. Naturally, we all followed suit.

"Normally a chest x-ray exposes the patient to 10 mrem. I'm getting 1000 mrem right now. The usual dosage for one year of exposure to natural ground and atmosphere radiation is a 300 mrem—over a whole year. Move back—way back!"

"So, there's a lot of radioactivity here. Is that what you're saying?" Picard insisted.

"I'm saying something in the ground has to have absorbed hundreds of thousands of rad to register 1000 mrem on this machine."

"Speak English, goddamit!" Picard yelled.

"It's probably the guy buried here is what I'm saying. He's highly radioactive—dangerously radioactive," the technician answered.

"Polonium," I said. "Robert was poisoned with polonium, just like me. Only he didn't get to a hospital in time."

"We're gonna have to dig him up to know that for sure, aren't we?" the FBI man queried. "I'll start the paperwork for a disinterment order as soon as we get back. We'll use a federal judge."

I knew that exhuming Robert would be useless. Where else could he have gotten all that radiation except from polonium? Besides, proving that Robert died from polonium poisoning would not prove who had poisoned him—or me, for that matter, and that is what I really wanted to find out. It would prove, however, that whoever the culprit was, he knew both of us. Trudy had found a reference to polonium on the UCC's server. That would be my starting point, but there was more than that I needed to learn. Where does Polonium come from? How would one of the most dangerous elements on the periodic chart get into anyone's hands? When I got back to Columbus, the first thing I did was call Trudy and ask her to go back into the ICC's server to see if there was anything else she could find on the subject. So what if it cost me another $1000. The second thing I did was start some of my own internet research about the element.

I learned that polonium is produced during the natural decay of uranium U-238. Due to its scarcity, polonium-210, however, is usually produced artificially in a nuclear reactor by bombarding bismuth-209 with a neutron. When ingested into the body by eating or drinking, 50% to 90% will promptly leave in the form of feces. Of what is left, 45% will be deposited in the spleen, liver and kidneys; 10% will be deposited in the bone marrow; and, the rest is distributed throughout the body's glands and lymph nodes. Polonium-210 poses no external risk when outside the body. But a 200 pound man who has ingested 0.9 micrograms of polonium-210 would have a median survival time of only 20 days. Polonium-210 is very rare, with only about 8 ounces being produced a year.

In minute amounts, polonium-210 also has commercial uses. For instance, it is used in brushes to clean dust particles from camera lenses and film, and it is used to eliminate static electricity from various machines that roll paper, spin synthetic fibers and manufacture plastic sheets. Its main commercial use is to eliminate static electricity.

But here are the facts that really caught my attention. Virtually all of the known production comes from a handful of Russian reactors. Russia produces it, and the United States buys virtually all of it in order to make sure that it doesn't leak into the black market. If a terrorist group or nation got its hands on any quantity of polonium, it could use it as an initiator for setting off a chain reaction in a crude nuclear bomb. So, maybe that's why there was an item on it in the ICC's server!

There are four facilities in Russia licensed to handle this substance: Moscow State University,

Techsnobexport, the state-controlled export agency, the Federal Nuclear Center in Samara, and Nuclon, a private company. I decided to have Trudy check out all four them, especially Nuclon, because it was private. This was going to cost me in the thousands with her, and I knew it, but if one of the names of these facilities appeared anywhere in the ICC computer, that could explain why there was a reference to polonium in their hard drive. Maybe Hamas, which was also on their hard drive, was trying to obtain the stuff as a trigger for some kind of "poor man's" nuclear device to be used somewhere—and maybe, just maybe the stuff had been used on Robert and me instead!

I called Trudy back and gave her the expanded assignment, and sure enough, I was right.

"It's gonna cost you close to five thousand bucks, big boy," she said. "It's a really big job."

"But, Trudes," I protested, "don't you want to help find out who poisoned me?"

"Only if I can thank them for helping you take off all that weight," she chided. "No, why should I even do it for that reason? What good is it to me that you've lost weight? It's the lovely Rosanne who should be thanking them, not me, and as for you, counselor, it's going to cost $5000 or no deal."

I knew what I could do to get Trudy's price down, but the thought of it was unacceptable. I couldn't bring myself to ask her out. What would Rosanne do if she ever found out? So I decided instead to try and interest her in all the intrigue surrounding polonium in the hopes that I could get her down to $2,500.

"OK, Trudes, twenty-five hundred it is. As an aside, let me tell you about a few interesting internet articles I also read about Alexander Litvinenko, the ex-lieutenant colonel in the KGB, who was thought to be the only case of known polonium poisoning that ever occurred—until me. There was also a rumor that polonium was used on a guy named Victor Yuschenko, the leader of the Orange Revolution in the Ukraine in 2004, which was about to wrest control away from a pro-Russian group supporting the current president in 2005."

After reading some of these articles to her, the curiosity got her price down, and it also got the better of me. I had heard the name Yuschenko before, and I had heard it somewhere locally, but where? I decided to waste a few minutes on an irrelevant search tracking him down.

So I accessed the *Columbus Dispatch* morgue on the internet, while Trudy was on the phone, looking for articles on Yuschenko. Voilà! A 2004 article appeared indicating that, of all people, Ekaterina Meltzer, in her role as an expert on Russian/Ukrainian foreign relations, had given a speech in Cleveland to the Ukrainian Society of Ohio, demonizing Yuschenko and supporting his opponent, Viktor Yanuchovych. The article indicated that she had close contacts with the pro-Russian government party of the Ukraine, run by Yanuchovich, almost to the unbelievable point of being an insider. This was the party Yuschenko was trying to bring down.

A few months after Ekaterina's speech, other articles appeared concerning the poisoning of Yuschenko, presumably with polonium, but it was later proven that a form of Agent Orange had been used. Yuschenko had not died, but he was seriously disfigured by the attempt to take his life with these chemicals. When I finished reading this stuff to Trudy, she was hooked. Her price came down to $2,500, "only because my interest is running so high now, counselor." The Yuschenko caper was all very interesting, but the other information I had found about polonium itself seemed far more relevant.

So, I told Trudy just to find any information she could on any communications between any of the four Russian polonium suppliers and the people at the ICC.

Chapter Twenty Five: Back in Court

"Mr. Barchrist gave me the letter and told me to put it in the Anthony Basheer file. I hadn't made up a new file on Mr. Basheer yet, so I put the letter on my desk, knowing it was important because it was signed by Mr. Steinglass, and Mr. Steinglass had just died—been killed that is. But I never got around to making up that file before it was time to leave for the evening. I knew it was important, but"—Marinda began sobbing—"but I didn't make the file before I left. I should have stayed over and done it." More sobbing. "I saw the letter each day I came in after that, laying there on my desk, waiting for my attention, and I meant to make a new file for it, but we got so busy." Now she was literally bawling out loud, tears dripping onto the glorious bare thighs partially revealed beneath her short electric yellow skirt. "Then we had the break-in, and I forgot about that letter completely until Mr. Barchrist asked me for it when he came to court last time."

"You had a break-in?" the judge asked.

"Yes, sir."

"My dear, are you saying the letter was purloined during the break-in? Is that it?" Judge Combtose's eyes never moved from her superbly tanned legs as he cross examined. He seemed to be paying little attention to the witness's answers.

"Well, I don't—"

"That's our position your honor!" I interrupted.

"know what 'purloined' means," Marinda continued.

"Huh? Oh, it means stolen," said the judge, losing patience. "Are you saying then that the letter from Robert Steinglass that would prove he had a will leaving his estate to Mr. Basheer was stolen when your office was broken into? That's what I'm asking you."

"That's our position," I reiterated, "and, when the person who broke in is discovered, there we'll find the letter!"

Suddenly, the mesmerizing effect of Marinda's thighs lost their grip on the judge, as he looked up and snapped, "Mr. Barchrist. Sit down! Let this witness answer! Now, please my dear, go ahead."

"Yes"

"Yes, what, my dear?"

"Yes. Yes to what Mr. Barchrist said."

Grudgingly the Judge snarled, "Well, Mr. Barchrist, have the police made any headway on identifying who broke into your office? I assume you called them."

"Yes, your honor, they have some evidence, an earring—in fact an earring that matches a set that was recently worn right in this very courtroom."

"Worn by whom, sir?"

"Worn by one of the parties to this case, your honor."

And with that all hell broke loose in the courtroom. Ekaterina Meltzer, who was the only other woman there, began screaming that I was using dirty, underhanded insulting tactics. Beside herself with rage, she shouted that I had previously accused her of withholding the partnership agreement between Stanley and Robert, that I had accused her of withholding Robert's will from Stanley's safe, and now I was having the gall to accuse her of breaking and entering. Her lawyer pointed his finger ferociously and began threatening a slander action. In the background, the judge gaveled for order to no avail and Tony snickered.

Marinda, still on the witness stand, utterly wailed throughout the fray. Even the reticent Boris, attached at the hip to his mother by an invisible towline Ekaterina kept around him when he was in court, began yelling. But Ekaterina quickly silenced him. Finally, the judge ordered the bailiff to get the police.

When order was restored, Judge Combtose excused Marinda from the stand and announced a decision. "This court will postpone this case for 90 days in order to give the police time to determine who broke into the offices of Winston Barchrist. Thereafter, I will hold a hearing to determine the intent of Stanley Meltzer with regard to the alleged partnership arrangement between Robert Steinglass and himself, and to determine the intent of Robert Steinglass with regard to the disposition of his estate."

"How can you do that? He's a bastard!" The words seemed to come out of nowhere. Quickly the judge gaveled for order, but they kept coming. "A bastard—just a bastard!

"Who's saying that?" the judge demanded.

Ekaterina was already hustling Boris out of the room, commanding him to shut his mouth. Once again the courtroom was in confusion. Was Boris calling the judge a bastard? Was he going to be held in contempt?

"Let him go, Ms. Meltzer," the judge commanded from the bench. "Now Mr. Meltzer, explain yourself! Who are you calling a bastard, sir?"

Wielding around and fighting to free himself from his mother's grasp, Boris answered, "Bobbi, my half brother, Bobbi Steinglass."

Ekaterina turned ashen. Her lawyer yelled out an objection. Tony let out an exhilarated "Aha!" and began laughing. Nonplussed, the judge ordered Stanley's son to explain himself again. Ekaterina's lawyer insisted, "Relevance, your honor. It's not relevant." But the judge was insistent. "I'm waiting, Mr. Meltzer. Explain yourself," he boomed.

Sheepishly, Boris answered, "Robert Steinglass was my father's bastard son. Nobody knew this except Robert, mother, father and me, and oh yes, Robert's real mother in Fremont, Ohio. Her name was Nessa Steinglass. They were never married, my father and her."

A long silence pervaded the courtroom. The lawyers for Ekaterina looked like deer blinded in someone's headlights. Marinda finally stopped crying. Ekaterina began muttering and swearing under her breath. Tony pinched my butt in glee. Finally Judge Combtose spoke.

"Well, Mr. Meltzer, if what you say is true, it certainly puts a whole new complexion on this matter. For one thing, at his death Mr. Steinglass may have had an interest in your father's law business, one way or the other—either as a partner, or as an heir. This is going to be a very complex case."

Ekaterina, who had regained her composure, now rose to address the court, her Ukrainian accent as thick as Texas crude oil.

"You know your honor, I vant you to remember three Russian proverbs vhen you are finally getting around to deciding this case. The first is, 'This is written vith a pitchfork on flowing vaters.' That describes Mr. Barchrist's position here. The second proverb is, 'Paper vill endure anything.' That's vhat I have, paper. I have a vill vith a pour-over trust that my husband left in his safe for me, and it says I get everything for my life and then my son Boris inherits everything. And the third proverb is, 'Law is like the shaft of a cart. It points vherever you turn it to.' This is the most important thing for you to remember Judge. Vhen you're dealing with the Stanley Meltzer Law Firm, you are dealing here with a forty million dollar estate. So, vhen you consider this last maxim, you must remember that in old Russia, carts were something only rich people owned and turned this way and that."

Chapter Twenty Six: Reflecting on Things

I didn't know what to make of Boris Meltzer's outburst. Robert Steinglass was Stanley Meltzer's son? Who would ever have expected that? Certainly, Robert had never let on to the fact. Nor could I imagine how or why it had been kept secret for so many years. Perhaps, this was Stanley's motivation for moving so quickly to erase any memory of Robert after his death. I knew from my luncheon at Ekaterina's house that Stanley was aware Robert had dealings with the Waqf, but the embarrassment that must have caused in front of their Jewish friends simply didn't seem to be a strong enough reason for obliterating all traces of him with such alacrity. Ekaterina had also made no bones about Robert's being gay, or about the relationship between him and Tony. Maybe that's why Stanley wanted to forget Robert so fast. But here was a stronger motive— proof of immorality on Stanley's part, certainly proof of impropriety, and maybe even infidelity! Robert was not just Stanley's son. He was his illegitimate son. That was certainly an embarrassment worth getting rid of as soon as the possibility presented itself.

Then there was the question of whether Stanley or Ekaterina knew anything about how Robert actually perished? That was doubtful. Obviously, al-Shabaab had killed Robert, either at Brucie's insistence or independently of it. Al-Shabaab had a strong motive for wanting to see him gone. He was working with the waqf against their interests, trying to thwart their lucrative sex trade in Somali women. Brucie, too, apparently had his reasons for wanting Robert dead, even though he claimed only to be trying to scare him. Robert was making noises about exposing Brucie's illegal business on North Bass Island. But why was Robert's grave ticking like Hiroshima in August of 1945? How did polonium figure into his death? As I was leaving the courthouse, my cell vibrated. It was Trudy. She hadn't found anything more in the ICC's computer files about polonium, except for some articles I'd already read about how it could be used to trigger a poor man's nuclear bomb. She'd also found an unsigned memorandum on why nuclear bombs didn't necessarily have to be destructive to terrorize.

"Did you ever think about it, Winston? Dirty bombs can cause as much terror by spreading radiation as destroying anything as large as the World Trade Center. Anyways, when I came up with so little that was specific, I felt I needed to do something more to earn my fee. So I started looking into the Yuschenko affair for you—not just general news articles, but into the hard drives of some of the players the articles named as being involved—and guess what?"

"You found out Yuschencko actually was poisoned with polonium, not Agent Orange."

"No, not exactly, but I found out somebody named Meltzer was involved."

"Yah, I already told you Ekaterina Meltzer gave a speech about the whole affair in Cleveland after it occurred."

"No, that wasn't it. The guy's name was Boris. Just thought there might be some outside chance of a connection."

"Boris? Boris Meltzer is Ekaterina Meltzer's son Trudy!"

"Well, Bingo! There, now I've earned my pay!"

"So what did you find? How was Boris Meltzer involved?"

"There was a bill of lading to a Russian company called Nuclon consigning a shipment of three kilograms of polonium to Boris Meltzer of the Kiev Polytechnic Institute, otherwise known as the National Technical University of Ukraine (NTUU). Meltzer was a research assistant in graduate school there. It sparked a brief investigation in Kiev concerning polonium as the poison possibly used on Yuschencko, before the toxicologists confirmed that the actual source of his poisoning was a dioxin similar to that used in Agent Orange."

"That doesn't add up, Trudy. My research indicated polonium-210 is a substance produced only by the Russians, who tightly control it, and most of it is bought up by the United States Defense Department, in order to keep it off the world market. It's only other use is for cleaning lenses and film, but for that, only minute quantities are needed. Why the Russians would allow this stuff into the Ukraine after the Ukraine became independent, just doesn't make any sense. Also, maybe this guy's a different Boris Meltzer. We need to find out more about Ekaterina's Boris Meltzer."

"I'm ahead of you on that one, boss. I've pulled up what I could on my screen while you were talking. I've only found two Boris Meltzers so far, without doing an extended computer search. One lives in Israel. The other's from—well, bust my booty—Bexley, Ohio! Now, if you'll just bear with me while I put my credit card in here, and I'll see what People Search comes up with on the "Bexley Boris." We'll do the most expensive search—all addresses, all known relatives, criminal record, jobs, education, etc. Ok, here we go— related to: Meltzer, Ekaterina L., Meltzer, Stanley, and two or three other Meltzers, probably uncles and aunts."

"What about his education? What does it say about that?"

"Education: Graduated, Ohio State University, 1995, Major physics, minors chemistry, and look at this—Russian; Masters Degree, 1997, Nuclear physics, National Technical University of Ukraine; doctoral studies with research in nuclear fission, National Technical University of Ukraine, 1998-2003; Ph.D. 2003."

"The Russian minor makes sense. His mother's an avid Russo-file. What about his employment?"

"Here it is: Arkon Laboratories, Columbus, Ohio, 2004 to present, formerly Director of Research: Polonium Aerosols; Author , *Cancer, Radiation and the Tobacco Industry; Teheran's Aborted Polonium Research*, and yadi, yadi, yada, many more. Do you want to hear all of them?"

"I don't think that'll be necessary, Trudes. So what you're telling me is this guy can get his hands on polonium whenever he wants it."

"I'm not saying that, boss. You are. All I'm saying is what the computer says about this guy. It's probably not easy for someone to get that stuff into or out of Arkon Labs without going to a lot of trouble. Besides, he's no longer into polonium aerosols. Now, he's directing something called the E4553 Gallimed Research Project."

I hung up convinced that Boris Meltzer had something to do with poisoning Robert. He surely had a motive. Robert was the darling of Stanley's law office, while Boris was Stanley's awkward scientific nerd son. Robert had told me how particular Stanley was about the way people looked and how they impressed other people. A man like Stanley would not have been proud of a son like Boris. Also, Robert stood to inherit from Stanley, which would cut into Boris' inheritance. Boris was a true heir and Robert was an inconvenient bastard. But what motive could Boris have had for slipping polonium-210, into *my* body and how could he have done it?

The starting point of my careful deduction concerning that issue had to be where and how I could have ingested the polonium. I don't smoke. So it couldn't have been through cigarettes. I don't remember being around any aerosols. So I had to have eaten it, but in what? I taxed my memory. What had we had for dinner that night in Cleveland at Imad's— lamb mixed with lentils, pita (more pita) and tabouli, with chocolate covered dates and black tea. I looked up the recipes on the computer. Translated, in addition to chopped lamb and lentil beans, I ate olive oil, garlic, lemon juice, crushed sesame seeds, lettuce, onion mint, parsley, tomatoes, flour and yeast. And for dessert, I had dates and tea. Awale easily could have slipped a little polonium into almost any of that stuff.

What had I had for lunch on that day? As I remembered it, that was the same day I'd eaten lunch at Ekaterina Meltzer's house. OMG! I'd had Mediterranean food for lunch too! She'd served dolmades, pita bread, cucumber salad, chick peas, dates and figs. Translated that was grape leaves with lamb or beef, cucumbers, and again, pita, chick peas and dates, as well as all the same spices.

So what had I eaten a lot of on that day? The answer was lamb, the spices, flour and dates. But if you count the chocolate covered dates from Brucie I took with me in the car to Cleveland, the food I'd eaten the most of was dates, with lamb and pita running close seconds. So, basically, this little exercise had left me nowhere. I'd eaten the same things everywhere I went on the day I was poisoned. I could have ingested the polonium at any point I had my big mouth open consuming food anywhere I ate on that day, including in my car on the way to Cleveland.

My bet was, it was the dates that carried the poison, because two of my suspects had fed me dates on the day I got sick—Brucie in the car, and someone at Imad's home. Awale was the most likely. He'd worked for Brucie, he'd worked for al-Shabaab, and he'd been in Imad's home when I was there. On the other hand, Brucie had also been connected to Robert before he'd become a ticking corpse, but there was no evidence linking Awale to Robert—at least not yet. And, there was certainly no evidence linking Boris Meltzer to Awale or to Brucie.

Of course, Ekaterina Meltzer had also served me dates on the day in question, and Boris Meltzer was certainly linked very closely with her. Could Ekaterina have poisoned me? There was only one way to find out, and that was to take a Geiger counter into her home looking for signs of radiation. If what I'd learned from the Litvinenko case was correct, there would be a polonium trail leading to anyone who had handled the stuff. That meant there would be traces of polonium in Ekaterina's home, in the kitchen or somewhere, if she had attempted to poison me with it.

But I'd need a search warrant to get a Geiger counter into Ekaterina's home, and Jerry Shapiro had already spoken on that subject, on behalf of the Columbus Police Department, by scoffing at my request that they get a warrant to search her home for the mate to the earring they'd found in my office. Of course, Jerry lacked the authority to do that, but he was right. There wasn't enough probable cause for a search warrant in that situation. And here, there was absolutely no probable cause for a search warrant to take a Geiger counter into Ekaterina Meltzer's home.

So, I reached a rather unconventional conclusion. Some "night work" was going to be necessary. I called Ronny.

"I don't know, boss," Ronny said. "You know I'd do anything for you. But that requires breaking and entering, and breaking and entering means breaking the law, and breaking the law to do that means big time jail time. Isn't there some other way to go on this? I mean I'd hate to have to explain how I got into Ekaterina Meltzer's home, let alone what I was doing there with a Geiger counter."

Ronny was right. We'd be hard pressed to use any evidence we found without having to explain how we found it. But, there had to be another way. Linking Boris, and his access to polonium, to Ekaterina was easy enough. The problem was showing that Ekaterina had used the substance in an attempt to kill me.

Maybe it was best to concentrate on the two most likely sources of my poisoning: first al-Shabaab, and second, Brucie. It was al-Shabaab that had the best motive for killing both Robert Steinglass and me. Brucie's motive was also pretty strong, but not quite as strong. How could he have gotten his hands on polonium-210 anyway? Furthermore, the link between Boris Meltzer and these two was non-existent. It was entirely speculative but I didn't care. I wasn't ready to give up yet on either al-Shabaab, Brucie, or now, Ekaterina.

Ronny was right. There had to be another way to implicate Ekaterina. We needed a search warrant, and there had to be a way the police could get one, even if it meant creating some facts. It was time for thinking out of the box.

Chapter Twenty Seven: In Pursuit of a Search Warrant

If you've never been in a Jewish cemetery, you should go just to experience the cultural difference. There aren't any crosses. There are no statues of angels, no chapels, no mausoleums, and all the gravestones have Hebrew letters on them that look like old bones etched into marble. It's daunting if you're not a Hebrew reader—quite an ancient feeling. There also aren't any columbariums or buried urns, because cremation isn't allowed, and if it's an Orthodox cemetery, as this one was, there aren't any non-Jews in the ground. Usually, Orthodox cemeteries are small, and not part of larger cemeteries, containing the remains of people from other denominations. Thus, they're unattended on any sort of a regular basis, somewhat run down and always in out of the way locales.

The Aguda Anshe Emmet burial ground was on a hill beside Alum Creek Boulevard near where a freeway overpass crossed the road. At night, headlights regularly scaling the grade up to the overpass flashed among the cemetery's mature poplar trees, creating a strobe-like effect that caused the Hebrew tombstones to flash on and off like something supernatural. It was eerie, not a very cozy place after dark. As we were scaling the iron fence protecting the place, Ronny produced a yarmulke and carefully placed it on his head.

"I didn't know you were Jewish, Ronny."

I'm not, boss. It's just out of respect." He struggled to get the Geiger counter equipment over the fence. "You know—it's the least I can do, given the situation. I feel like we're grave robbing."

I looked down at the note Rabbi Billy had given me, and flipped on my flashlight. This wasn't going to be easy. There was no English on many of the gravestones, and definitely there was no English on the metal markers marking the fresh graves awaiting the erection of head stones. Everything was in Hebrew. So Billy had written out Stanley Meltzer's Hebrew name for me, carefully printing each letter. I bent down comparing what was on the paper to what was on one of the metal markers, but nothing seemed to match.

"Ronny, I can't make heads or tails out of this. It's all Greek to me. None of the letters on this paper match any of these markers."

"That's because Hebrew is read from right to left, but you're reading it from left to right, boss," he answered. "Here give me that." He bent down and began matching up the characters on Billy's note to the markers from right to left. "Yah, this is the one," he said looking up. "This is Stanley Meltzer's newly dug grave."

"Ronny, are you sure you're not Jewish?

"No, I'm Greek, man, through and through. My last name is Herimus, remember? But Ancient Greek is written from right to left, just like Hebrew, and my mother used to drag me to Greek Orthodox services on Easter at St. Philothea's. While I was there, I learned which way the ancient Greek alphabet goes. That's where I learned that you're supposed to respect the dead too. So, I brought a skull cap."

"Fine, let's just do what we came here to do and get out of here." I began fitting the boom into the

Geiger counter so Ronny could wand Stanley's grave. I planned to stand close by watching over his shoulder to note down the level of any ticking we got. He was busy dressing in the protective gear he'd brought along to ward off radiation exposure, which he greatly feared. "Where'd you get the crazy idea this grave would be radioactive anyways," he whined.

"I didn't. I just figured that if Boris Meltzer was around his mother with any polonium-210, there could be traces of the stuff on her, and if she was around his father, well, there might be feint traces on him too. So I thought maybe we ought to test out Stanley's grave, just for "shits and giggles." Of course, we're just talking traces, so I don't expect any big readings, certainly not enough to warrant all that protective equipment you're wearing."

"So we're just looking for a few ticks, and if we get 'em, we can leave, right, boss?"

"Right, Ronny, right. Don't be so worried. You ready?"

Ronny moved the boom to the center of the little hill of fresh earth piled in a rectangle extending from the metal marker. No grass had grown over it yet. He placed the ring at the end of the boom over what I figured to be Stanley's abdomen. I had re-charged the Geiger Counter from a car battery, hoping to make it strong enough to pick up any hint of radiation that was above the norm. Ronny looked back at me, and I gave him the nod to turn on the machine.

Instantly, there was an explosion of pocks! They strengthened as he moved the wand down the grave toward where Stanley's lower abdomen should have been. It was the same incessant ticking we'd experienced at Robert's grave in Fremont when I was up there checking it for radiation with the police.

"Let's get out of here," I yelled as we both jumped back from the grave.

"Did you get a reading?" Ronny asked.

"No, the whole thing was too shocking. I forgot."

"No problem, boss," he said, as he adjusted his protective gear and waded into the midst of the ever increasing pocking to record radiation levels. "Not only do I have this protective gear, but I'm wearing a yarmulke I should be fine."

The next day I called the Columbus Police Department to ask for a meeting with Antoine Picard. The issue of who had killed Robert had not been definitively solved yet, and my plan was to convince the detective there was a link between Ekaterina Meltzer and Robert's death by explaining her son's access to the element of polonium-210 and his history of handling the substance during his graduate years in the Ukraine and during his professional years at Arkon Labs.

At the meeting, just as I had planned, I sprang my *coup de gras* on them. I had discovered Stanley's grave ticking as loudly as Robert's had been the day we were all at the Fremont Cemetery together and, as I saw it, the next step of the police would have to be the application for a search warrant to examine Ekaterina Meltzer's home for traces of polonium. While they were at her residence, they could also look for the mate to the earring they'd found in my office after the break-in.

"What is it with you and cemeteries?" Shapiro quipped. He'd been asked by Detective Picard to sit in on the meeting. "Haven't you got anything else to do but traipse around graves with Geiger Counters? You know, most cemeteries are classified as private property."

"Well, you can arrest me for trespassing if you want, Jerry," I shot back exasperatedly. "But the fact remains. You now have evidence that links Ekaterina Meltzer to the unsolved murder of Robert Steinglass, as well as to what was obviously the murder of her husband. So if you don't want to act on it, there's nothing I can do, but I suggest that you get a search warrant!"

"No it doesn't—"

"No it doesn't what?

"link Ekaterina to the murder of Robert Steinglass, or to the demise of Stanley Meltzer. Your evidence links Boris Meltzer to those two deaths, not Ekaterina. Boris was the one with the motive. After his mother, he stood to inherit all Stanley's wealth."

Picard was nodding his agreement with Jerry's conclusion. Had I jumped too fast? Was there still no probable cause to search Ekaterina Meltzer's home? What had I left out? Then it came to me.

"Yah, *after* his mother," I reminded them. "First she was going to inherit, but what about my case? The only people who could have attempted to murder me with polonium were people who fed it to me, and the only people who fed me anything on the day I got sick were the people at the home of Dr. Imad al-Katib in Cleveland, Lloyd Bruce, who sent me chocolate covered dates, and Ekaterina Meltzer, who fed me lunch. I had lunch at her home on the day I got sick! I don't think you ever knew that.

Boris never gave me any food. The only time I've ever seen him was in court, and then he was always sitting at a table on the other side of the room. So if that doesn't raise any doubt in your minds about Ekaterina Meltzer, I don't know what will."

Picard looked at Shapiro. "OK, Jerry," he said. "Let's go interview Boris Meltzer about his access to polonium. I want to know when the last time was that he worked with it in this country, and how he gets it when he works with it. Come to think of it, maybe we should have the Feds question him on those subjects. I'm sure its importation is carefully controlled by our customs people." With that, the two of them pushed back their chairs.

"Well, what about the warrant?" I insisted.

"Not yet," Picard answered.

"What motive did Ekaterina Meltzer have to poison you?" Shapiro asked.

Chapter Twenty Eight: Thinking Inside the Box

To prove the crime of first degree murder, or attempted first degree murder, the best things the prosecution can have, in the absence of an eye witness, are: the weapon, a body, a suspect with access to the weapon and a motive, and, evidence of the suspect's malice of forethought. In my case, we had the weapon, polonium. We had the body, me, and we also had three suspects, two of whom had motives but no access to the weapon, and the third of whom may have had access to the weapon. But what could Ekaterina's motive have been?

Awale worked for al-Shabaab, which had a motive for wanting me dead—my ties to the waqf—but no provable access to polonium; and Brucie had a motive——my knowledge of his North Bass Island operation——and he had certainly demonstrated his malice by kidnapping Rosanne, but he also had no provable access to polonium. Ekaterina may have had provable access to the weapon, but what was her motive, and where was the proof of her malice aforethought?

The police were about to investigate Boris' access to the weapon, but it looked like tying Ekaterina to polonium-210 and proving her motive and malice aforethought were going to be left up to me. Since I couldn't get into her house, there was only one place left to look, Boris. I called Trudy.

"This time I'm way ahead of you, boss. I was just getting ready to call you. When the Boris Meltzer I found turned out to be living in Bexley, I got real curious. So I decided to donate some of my not so copious free time to your cause. I broke into Nuclon's computer—in Russia, you know, the only private polonium producer in Russia. Believe me, it wasn't so easy—and I found a shipping manifest, dated last month, from that company for polonium to a consignee named Arkon, c/o Dr. B. Malcoff. It went to a post office box in Columbus, Ohio. So I made a copy and I went down to the main post office and checked it out. Guess what? Arkon doesn't have any P.O. Box with that number in Columbus. Neither does a Dr. B. Malcoff. So what do you make of that?"

"What do I make of that? I make of it that it's time to have Arkon call the office of the Postal Inspector and complain that somebody's using a box with that number under their name. That's what I make of that."

"How we gonna do that, boss, without exposing me to criminal charges for computer hacking?"

"We're going to do it with just you and me, Trudes––without Arkon ever knowing what you've done."

***

The Office of the Inspector General had a fogged glass door with the words *United States Post Office, Office of Inspector General*, across it in plain black print, opening off a cavernous hallway in the Main Post Office. Inside were two wooden chairs facing another door, this one solid wood, with no lettering on it. Except for the tattoo of a black rose on her thigh, Trudy looked very much the professional business woman, sitting beside me, legs crossed in her black skirt, white blouse and matching black jacket.

"Mr. Sensenbrenner can see you now for five minutes," snapped the Black fiftyish looking woman who suddenly appeared from behind the inner door. She took in Trudy's tattoo and sneered, while opening the door wider to allow us to pass. Inside, sitting at a desk in a white shirt and colorless tie, was another Black woman, wearing glasses with brown rectangular frames and coke-bottle lenses. "You can sit there," the women spat in a bossy tone, pointing to two wooden chairs and with that she left, slamming the door.

"Ms. Lewis is having a bit of a difficult day," Mr. Sensenbrenner said, apologizing for her. "What can I do you for?"

"We're here from Arkon Laboratories' Institute," Trudy began. I'm Miss Fischel and this is our lawyer Mr. Barchrist." With that, I handed the man my card. "I'm afraid we've discovered a discrepancy that may involve postal fraud." She handed a copy of the manifest and the bill of lading for the recent shipment of polonium to Mr. Sensenbrenner. "Are you familiar with the element called polonium?"

"I'm afraid not."

"It's a highly unstable radioactive substance that is tightly controlled by the government," she continued. "We believe someone is buying minimal quantities of this element from this Russian manufacturer, Nuclon, and taking shipments of the stuff, falsely under our auspices, at the post office box number mentioned in these papers. Arkon has no such post office box. We also have nobody named Malcoff," she added, unknowingly.

"How did you come across this information?" the inspector asked.

"We're not at liberty to divulge that to you," I interrupted, "Attorney-client privilege."

"We need to know who rents this box," Trudy continued.

"And I'm afraid I'm not at liberty to divulge that to you," the Inspector retorted, "Privacy Act won't allow it these days, and even if it did, the good ol' P.O. would never do a thing like that—too far below the moral high ground, integrity of the system—you know.

We can certainly find out who rents the box, though, and if they're using your company's name in connection with a box number that's not yours, that could be mail fraud. We'd have to get a warrant to open the box. But we have the power to investigate for fraud, you know, and we like to use it. Use it or lose it, as they say." Then the smile of an insider creased his face. "And in doing so we can certainly contact you, perhaps with a contrived list of names to find out if any of the listed people work for you and who they are. That's all within our regulations, bureaucratic bullshit and such— you know."

"That'll work," said Trudy. Please contact Mr. Barchrist here when you have your list ready."

With that, the inspector buzzed his angry Black assistant, and she showed us out, the whole way glaring at Trudy's thigh. "I don't know why they call him an inspector," Trudy said under her breath, when the woman finally broke off our escort. "With those glasses, I doubt he could inspect anything very well. He's practically blind."

Chapter Twenty Nine: The List

"The Postal Inspector finished checking out who rented our suspect Post Office box, and I got the list of possible renters from him today. Guess who was on it?" I was talking to Trudy on my office phone.

"Boris Meltzer?"

"You got it!"

"What are you gonna do?"

"I've already done it. Picard and Shapiro were very interested when I met with them to explain what we'd done. Of course, Jerry gave me his usual crap about leaving police work up to the cops, but they eagerly went out to the cemetery with a Geiger counter after the meeting to listen to Stanley Meltzer's grave, and they came back, ready to ask the Department to request search warrants for the residences of both living Meltzers."

"You didn't tell them I was involved, did you?"

"Not by name."

She laughed. "Did you tell them to go to Judge Combtose for the warrants? That would be only fitting, wouldn't it?"

"Yah, but they're going Federal. That means they'll go through the Post Office to a Federal judge because of the mail fraud charges the Inspector General decided to bring against Boris when I told him Boris was the only one on the list who worked for Arkon Labs."

"Is that true?"

"Is what true?"

"He's the only one who works for Arkon on the list?"

"Who knows?"

"Well, what if you're wrong?"

"If I'm wrong, I don't know. I'll lose all credibility with the Police Department and the Post Office might stop delivering my mail. Who knows? But they can't do much else to me. I didn't give anyone an affidavit that Boris was the only one on the list working for Arkon."

"And what about pretending to be Arkon's lawyer in front of the Inspector General?"

I suppose that's just one of those things we'll have to leave to the interstices of the law."

"What are those?"

"Never mind, Trudes. Suffice it to say they have something to do with the Supreme Court's right of privacy decisions. It's a Constitutional thing. In any event, I'd like to be a fly on Ekaterina's wall when they serve the warrant on her. She's got a hot temper. They're going in today on the warrant request, and they'll be serving the warrants by Friday. "

"Well, do you anticipate there'd be any problems with the warrants if your little charade as Arkon's lawyer came to light?"

"I doubt that's going to happen, Trudes. At this point, things are looking really good for us. The great polonium mystery is about to be cracked wide open. I'm sure of it."

As I hung up, Marinda poked her head in the door telling me Jerry Shapiro was on the other line, and not sounding very happy. *Oh, crap,* I thought to myself. *That busy body little cop has gone and called Arkon about the whole thing, and they told him they'd never heard of me.* I picked up the other line ever so tentatively.

"Yah, Jerry?"

"We got the warrant to search Boris Meltzer's place, but the judge said no for now to the one for Ekaterina Meltzer's home. He said they're just isn't enough probable cause—that is it's not more probable than not that a connection between her and the death of her husband or Steinglass exists. And he doesn't see any connection between what happened to you and her either."

"Jerry, that's terrible. "What about the polonium you found at Meltzer's grave? What about the fact that she fed me lunch on the day I got sick? I thought we were talking murder or attempted murder charges here?"

"There you go again, counselor," he answered doing his favorite imitation of Ronald Reagan, "jumping the gun. What part of "no" don't you understand? There's no evidence the ticks and pocks we heard in that Orthodox Jewish cemetery were polonium. For all we know, Stanley Meltzer ate some radio-active lox with his bagels before he died. We finally got an autopsy proving Steinglass died from polonium poisoning, but we don't have one for Meltzer, and it's not gonna be easy getting an order to dig him up if that harpy wife of his finds out that's what we want to do."

"What part of 'no' don't I get? I don't understand the no 'for now' part. What does that mean? What does 'for now' mean? What else does the judge want?"

"Well, he recommended we seek a FISA Warrant from the FISC, instead of coming back to him."

"What's a FISA warrant? What's the FISC?"

"FISC stands for the United States Foreign Intelligence Court, which is a Federal Court established under the Foreign Intelligence Surveillance Act. A FISA Warrant is a surveillance warrant. The FISC sits in Washington D.C. We've already contacted the Attorney General's Office about an appointment with them."

Surveillance! We don't need surveillance, I thought to myself. *We need to search her house and to get a Geiger counter in there.* "How is this a national security matter?" I asked.

"It's because of the polonium," Shapiro said. "Did you know you can make nuclear bomb triggers with that stuff?"

"Yah, I knew, but how did you know? Who brought it up when the warrant was requested?"

"I did. I looked it up, and I told the judge, just to strengthen our case a little, and it did—on Boris' warrant at least."

"That's just great, Jerry. How long will it take to get a FISA Warrant?"

"About 30 days, maybe 45."

"Oh, so now I get it. 'No, not yet' means the federal judge here was friendly with Stanley Meltzer and his wife, just like all the other judges in town. He's kicking the can down the road because he doesn't want to be involved."

"So go do me something, counselor. That was the decision. Get over it! Tell you what, since I know how disappointed you are, you can come with us when we serve Boris's warrant on him and search his place. Would you like that?"

"I'll be there."

***

The entry into Boris's apartment went smoothly. He just seemed disoriented when the entourage of police and marshals broached his doorway and waived the warrant at him. He read it; curled his lips, shaking his head and then he just let everyone in right away. He claimed he hadn't worked with polonium-210 for over a year and that if there were any traces of the stuff around they'd most likely be at the lab, not in his home.

He was cordial, explaining his research with polonium, what it can be used for in industry, and the various properties of the element—helpful, that is, until his Miranda Rights were read to him and questions began flying about the Post Office box he'd rented. Then he soured and demanded to speak with an attorney before saying anything else.

"I have no idea who was using my name to rent that box. I can assure you it wasn't me."

But instead of calling an attorney, he went into the other room and called his mother, who must have scared him speechless. We could hear her yelling at him through the phone, but not what she was saying. He hung up and never said another word.

He was arrested on charges of mail fraud, taken to the police station, and slated pending indictment proceedings before the Grand Jury. Sans the tutelage of his mother at the station, and realizing he was going to be sleeping there at least for the night because there would be no bail hearing until the morning, in exchange for the promise of a private cell and some carry-out Chinese from Wings Restaurant out in Bexley, he admitted having been inside his mother's home with a quantity of polonium, but would not reveal why, when, or how much of the substance was involved. He simply refused to say another word about it after the Chinese food arrived.

After his bail hearing the next day, his mother immediately posted bond. Ekaterina was "hoppin' mad," as they say. That afternoon the police showed up at her door just to ask a few questions, but without any warrant, and, according to Jerry Shapiro, her reaction was something close to George Wallace's 1963 stand-off at the University of Alabama's Enrollment Center Doors. Not only did she not invite them in, but as soon as the words "polonium-210" were mentioned, she called her lawyer on her cell phone, right from her doorway. She also claimed something close to diplomatic immunity and called the Russian Consulate in Cleveland. Then she punched her speed dial number for Judge Combtose, invoked their friendship, the size of the Meltzer name in the community, and she screamed at him to do something about the invasion of her privacy by the police. "She seemed to be blaming him for the police being at her door because he had postponed some sort of will contest case to allow us to determine who may have broken into your office," Jerry reported.

The judge's voice could be heard vibrating on Ekaterina's cell, and he talked to her for what seemed an extremely long time. Apparently her voice began to ripple as she spoke to him. Then, suddenly she burst into flame.

"That's it? There's nothing *you* can do?" she yelled.

Flabbergasted by his impotence to intervene in the situation that had unfolded at her front door, she threw her cell phone into the yard.

"She glared at us and turned her eyes toward the sky as if remembering her lines. 'If you have no varrant and you have no subpoena, I don't have to speak to you and I von't. Please leave my property—right now!'"

So, as Jerry tells it, the police returned to the cruiser. "I said we should arrest her," he opined. "But Picard said no."

"On what grounds?" he asked. "Disturbing the peace?"

Then, Jerry began imitating her. "If you have no charges against me, and no legal papers that say I must talk vith you, and no subpoena, I vant you to leave. I vant you to leave right now!" He mimicked, adding, "Even I was a little frightened of her."

Chapter Thirty: Surprise Visitor

Two weeks later, sitting alone in my office with my feet up, contemplating the damage Ohio State's latest football scandal was doing to the university's football program, I heard the outer door to my waiting room opening. No one was expected, and it was one of Marinda's off-days. Weighing the relative merits of getting up against the serenity of just staying seated in my inner sanctum, hoping whoever it was would leave—future new business versus present personal comfort—I decided to go out and greet whoever it was.

There, standing in the outer office was Ekaterina Meltzer, dressed in a revealing low cut black dress, with a brightly colored cotton jacket over her shoulders, holding a large Gucci bag. Once again, no stockings—just bear legs in high heels. Casually, almost nonchalantly, she withdrew a Glock 19, with silencer attached, from the Gucci, and pointed it at me. She reached behind herself and locked the door.

My mind blanked momentarily. Here was the succubus I had imagined, ready to draw blood. Would she just fire? Or did she want to talk first?

"Mrs. Meltzer," I heard myself saying. "Welcome. The necklace you're wearing matches an earring that was found here by the police."

"Vell, that's neither here nor there anymore, isn't it, Mr. Barchrist?"

"And why do you say that?"

"Because in just a moment that little Vill contest suit you filed against me is going to be over, at least for you."

"But Judge Combtose said he wasn't going to be ruling on anything until the police had time to figure out who broke into my office."

Her jaw muscles tightened and her eyes spit fire. "That judge is an idiot," she snarled through clenched teeth, and she raised the gun a little higher. "They've had enough time."

I thought she was going to fire right then and there. Holding up my hand, I yelled, "Wait! If that's what this is all about, I mean the will contest, I'm sure we can work something out, a settlement, maybe, that's very advantageous to you—something that results in an end to the case without raising any more questions about the relationship between your late husband and Robert Steinglass."

"Vhy did you go and get my Boris into trouble?"

"Me?"

"Don't lie to me, Mr. Barchrist. I had a little chat vith them over at Arkon Labs. You passed yourself off vith the Post Office as their attorney to find out who rented the Postal Box. They don't even know who you are! You snooped into my son's career, into his dealings vith Nuclon Corporation in Russia. You told the Inspector General Boris was using the mail to take deliveries of polonium. Vhy on earth vould you do such a thing? Because of that little fairy ballet dancer Bob called his vife? You're trying to take my son's rightful inheritance avay from him!"

"It's your inheritance too, and I'm not trying to take it."

"Vhy? You are meddling in things that are not your business, Mr. Barchrist!" Vhy?"

She used the word "things" in the plural. Maybe there was more at stake in her mind than just the will contest action.

"What do you mean *things?"* I asked.

"Don't get cute vith me, Mr. Barchrist. Vhat suddenly is this big interest of yours in polonium? Tell me."

Apparently, the folks at Arkon had revealed everything I'd told the Inspector General. It sounded like the jig was up as far as she was concerned. *Just keep her talking*, I thought. *Something might happen that changes this situation before she can shoot.*

"Maybe it's because you tried to poison me with polonium-210. Maybe it's because you actually did poison Robert Steinglass. Maybe it's because you killed your own husband," I said in a quavering voice.

Suddenly, a tinkling sound of metal against metal sounded just behind her as the mail came through the slot in the door and slapped onto the floor. It diverted her attention just long enough for me to lunge at her pistol. Angrily, she fired into the ceiling twice; shed her Gucci bag; and reached around my neck with her other arm. I took her down, but she was a lot stronger than I thought. Sinewy legs came out of her hiked up black dress; wrapped around my poloniumized torso and began crushing my ribs. I felt something give in my chest, and a splitting pain shoot up my side to the arm I was using to pin back her gun. I let go. I was thinner from the polonium, but also weaker, especially in my bones and upper body. Furiously, she began whipping me in the face with the pistol, making my brains spin, but on one of her swipes somehow I managed to grab the gun away from her. Bleary eyed and unable to get up, I watched from the floor as she unlocked the door and disappeared.

The next thing I remembered was looking up at the clerk from the Dairy Mart beneath my office.

"What the hell is going on up here? he asked, wide-eyed. "Sounded like a sumo match or something from downstairs."

"Call the police," I coughed, pointing to the two bullet holes in the ceiling. The guy looked up at the ceiling squinting with a questioning look in his eyes.

"Bullets," I wheezed. "Silencer."

Shapiro arrived within minutes. He looked at the bullet holes. He looked at the blood all over my face, and he was no longer his usual cocky self.

"It was Ekaterina Meltzer," I said. He radioed into the station asking for an "all points bulletin" on her immediately.

"We'll get her, Win. We'll pick her up. Now tell me what happened."

Chapter Thirty One: The Melt Down

They didn't...pick Ekaterina up, that is. It turned out that she'd pre-purchased a one way ticket on Delta to New York, departing Columbus an hour and a half after she left my office. She had a connecting flight to Moscow, leaving at 5:00 p.m. from JFK. The Russian Consulate in Cleveland had issued her a visa just two days before.

The airport police missed her at the Columbus airport, and by the time the cops at JFK were contacted, she was already in the air to Russia. Upon landing at Domedodovo International outside Moscow, she immediately applied for Russian citizenship, citing the former Soviet Union as the land of her birth because the Ukraine was a part of the U.S.S.R. when she was born. An extradition application was filed, but it's still making its way through the Russian bureaucracy because of, among other things, her citizenship application.

Nonetheless, she has pursued her former husband's estate from Moscow. Judge Combtose, of course, has been willing to oblige her despite her absence from the country, and despite the charges of assault with a deadly weapon which have been filed against her.

"Only matters of inheritance are within the purview of this Court, not criminal matters," he exclaimed during a recent hearing, still afraid of her and the sway of the Meltzer name in the community. His term is about to expire—not a good time to risk making enemies among the voting public.

Thirty days after Ekaterina left the country, Boris Meltzer was indicted on one count of mail fraud. The offense carries a sentence of up to five years in a federal penitentiary for individuals and a fine of up to $250,000 dollars. On the advice of counsel, he agreed to provide information during plea bargaining negotiations. The Attorney General refused any deal unless Boris came clean on whether he had illegally imported polonium. He admitted he had, but when asked what he was doing with it, he said, "Really, nothing at all. I gave it all to my mother, and showed her how to handle it. She was the one who told me to rent the post office box and to contact Nuclon."

"Do you always do what your mother says?" the Attorney General quipped.

"Do you know my mother?" he replied.

"Well, what did she do with it?"

"I don't know. I truly don't know. She said she wanted to use it for removing dust in a film processing business she was backing as a start-up company. She was never really clear about it."

Picard was certain this was a lie. By this time, the Columbus police had secured an order to disinter Stanley Meltzer. There was an autopsy, and the county coroner ruled that polonium poisoning was the cause of his death. Boris was shocked to hear this. He maintained he'd had nothing to do with it, realizing that his denials were implicating his mother. "I don't believe mother would do such a thing either," he whimpered.

When the Attorney General asked if he knew anything about what caused Robert's death, he denied having any knowledge. On the advice of counsel, he agreed to take a lie detector test concerning his roles, if any, in both deaths. He passed. As he had maintained, he had no knowledge and no involvement. He pled guilty to one count of mail fraud, was given a one year sentence and fined $25,000 dollars.

The best thing to come out of Boris's mail fraud case, as far as I was concerned, was his admission to having placed his mother in possession of polonium-210. Based on that statement, the Columbus Police Department was able to obtain a search warrant to search Ekaterina's house. By this time, the traces of radiation that were found in her kitchen, bathroom and basement were substantially weaker than those found at the grave sites of Stanley and Robert, due to polonium-210's half life, but still strong enough to reveal that the substance had been present in her home. The police also retrieved the match to the earring unearthed in my office after the break-in. Presumably, Ekaterina had worn the necklace part of the set on her plane trip to Russia. Warrants for her arrest on murder and attempted murder charges were added to the outstanding arrest warrant for assault with a deadly weapon that had already been filed against her.

But there was also something else found in her home, an envelope addressed in the handwriting of Robert Steinglass to Anthony Basheer. Inside it was Robert's letter to Tony chastising him for refusing to accept a copy of the missing will he'd placed in the safe at the Stanley Meltzer Law Offices. It was the same letter Marinda had negligently allowed to lie around on her desk for days without filing it. It was the "purloined" document, and she is now able to testify clearly to that. If staring down at her crossed legs as she testifies fails to remove all concern for his re-election from Judge Combtose's mind, and he finds some other reason to put off the trial to accommodate Ekaterina's side of the story, or Boris' prison time, I plan to move that he be replaced by another judge. After all, a murderer cannot inherit from the person whom she murdered in Ohio, and we don't want the estate going to the State of Ohio because Boris is in federal prison.

After Tony authenticates the letter, the judge should quickly rule that his will contest action can proceed. Thereafter, Tony should wind up with not only his fair share of the receipts due Stanley Meltzer as of the day of his death and Robert's invested capital invested in the firm, but also Robert's undivided half share in North Bass Island, which will be sold for cash after certain other legal proceedings occur, namely the disposition of the charges against Lloyd Bruce.

Lloyd (Brucie) Bruce was indicted for growing unlawful substances, possession of marijuana, drug trafficking, transportation of illegal substances, conspiring with al-Shabaab to engage in terrorist activity, and providing material support to a terrorist organization. He is currently in jail without bond because of the terrorism counts. His federal trial is scheduled for next year, and he is attempting to plea bargain for reduced charges by cooperating with the authorities concerning information about al-Shabaab's operations in the Midwest. If plea bargain negotiations are successfully concluded, he will no doubt be put in a federal penitentiary for a period of time, and North Bass Island will be sold while he's there, in order to pay his attorneys and Tony Basheer. In the meantime, the state of Ohio is pursuing his indictment for kidnapping in the second degree, which carries a sentence of up to eight years in State prison after his federal stint is over. The State is pursuing a second degree felony, rather than a felony in the first degree, because Brucie's thugs released Rosanne unharmed.

Harold and Ludmilla the vixen somehow escaped from jail in Sandusky, Ohio, and disappeared. Shortly thereafter, Brucie's 39-foot Sea Ray-Sundance was found missing from its slip at Put-In-Bay and turned up beached near Port Dover, Canada. So far, Harold and Ludmilla haven't been found.

Awale, the servant in Imad's house, and later the employee of Josh Shackman, pled guilty to being a member of a terrorist organization, and he is currently residing at a maximum security facility in Colorado dubbed the "Supermax." He is dreading deportation once his sentence has been served, and has contacted me about seeking naturalization as a citizen of the United States, another one of those uncomfortable legal engagements that continue to un-enhance my legal reputation with the Columbus Bar.

As for me, I continue, as the trustee for the *The Waqf al Columbus Somali,* the trust Robert was trying to set up for the benefit of Somali refugees living in Columbus before he died. Another money order from *La Banque Postale* has rolled in since Robert's death, bringing the corpus of that trust to a cool $10,000,000. I can't tell you what my trustee's fees are, but suffice it to say Marinda is now full-time, I have increased my staff, and to make room for them, I have now expanded into the office space next door, which is over the optometrist's office downstairs beside the Dairy Mart. So far, we've funded a Muslim Family Services Program for the Somali Community, funded regular English classes and a small sports center in the Somali neighborhood, and set up a "Somali Elders' Organization" to counsel with the police department concerning crime in the Somali community, which hopefully, will block further al-Shabaab activities.

Oh, and Josh Shackman has now thrown much of his collection activity and the landlord tenant work for Shackman Industries my way. Rosanne and I have begun regularly attending the Synagogue he built on Saturdays, even though I'm not Jewish. Rabbi Billy's delighted. Rosanne is making plans to spend my attorney's fees for Tony's probate matter on a trip for her, Gayna and me to the Bahamas—that's assuming we win the case of course.

The End

ABOUT THE AUTHOR

David M. Selcer authors the Buckeye Barrister mystery
 series, the first of which was
DEADLY AUDIT. After graduating
from Northwestern University, Selcer
attended Ohio State University Law
School. He then had an exciting career
practicing management labor law with
a large national law firm for 35 years.
Today, he has retired to Sarasota,
Florida, where he feels his job is either to sleep or to
write mysteries. Somewhere along the line, he helped
raise five kids. He also still manages to make decisions
on employment cases involving the Post Office as a
Federal Agency Decision Writer. He is an avid OSU
Buckeye fan.

www.ingramcontent.com/pod-product-compliance
Lightning Source LLC
Chambersburg PA
CBHW020326260626
47156CB00004B/1401